# The

# Curate Barley

# Mysteries

## By

## TE HODDEN

For Michelle

# THE WEB OF DECEIT

# ONE

Friday morning started early. Mrs Wimslow from Tannery Road didn't even wait for me to finish making my coffee to give me one of her little calls. My phone shimmied on the kitchen counter and made me regret choosing such a perky ringtone. It had seemed like a good idea.

I groaned, gritted my teeth, and tried to make my voice sound like I was smiling. "Maureen," I said, with as much cheer as I could muster. "Is... everything okay?"

"Tabitha has done it again," Mrs Wimslow said.

"Oh," I sighed.

"She tricked me!" Mrs Wimslow spluttered. Sullenly she added. "Again."

"Right." I rubbed the back of my head. "And... you have tried everything the nice man from the RSPCA suggested?"

"She's mocking me," Mrs Wimslow insisted.

I held the sigh in, until after I had promised to head right over, and hung up the phone. Then I let out a breath that came dangerously close to unbecoming language and fought the urge to smack myself in the face with a cupboard door. The moment passed. I buttoned up my shirt and slipped the dog collar on. It almost covered the scar on my throat. Almost, but not quite. Enough not to notice.

I made it out of my flat, and was almost at the stairs, before the door across the way opened, and Helen leant out from her apartment to call after me.

"Hey! Barley!" she cooed.

I stopped, straightened my back, squared my shoulders and by some miracle was looking more human than zombie by the time I had turned around to face her.

Helen was quite possibly the most beautiful person I had ever met. She was a few years younger than me, a single mother of two little whirlwinds in primary school uniforms, a larger woman, with ample curves, and a smile that could hit you from a hundred paces. She had latte skin, mocha hair, and chestnut eyes full of mischief and laughter.

"Hi," I said.

"Hey," Helen said, colour flushing her cheeks. "So... you know that dating app I said I was trying? It... kind of works... and..."

"And?" I asked, tentatively.

She toyed with a curl of her hair. "And... I don't suppose you would be free Friday night? To watch the Trouble?"

"I certainly can be," I promised. "Did you want to drop them at mine?"

"Or, would you mind stepping over to mine for a few hours?" She batted her eyes. "The kids will be fed, and settled, and they won't be up for too long, so..."

"What time?" I asked.

"Six?" she asked, hopefully.

I nodded. "Sure. Absolutely."

Her smile brightened, and I left the building with the fuzzy glow of that smile. The one that made you think you had always been her best friend, even before she ever happened to meet you.

*

A twenty-five-minute, rush hour tube ride later, I was stood in the shadow of Cinderoak, the largest of the concrete tower blocks in the Gallow Cross parish. It was a blunt faced monolith, a surviving remnant of what the nineteen fifties thought the year two thousand would look like, now scuffed, weathered, and saggy around the seams, peppered with little acts of mindless vandalism, and graffiti. None of it was the artistic kind, with any talent, or redeeming beauty. The one wall where a frustrated artist had left a mural had been daubed over with the rancid blatherings of who shagged who, or ate what, or was a such a such. The mirrored wall of the elevator had been carved with the word "wanker" scratched deep into the glass.

I rode the lift to the sixteenth floor and stepped out onto the balcony walkway.

The view of the parish, of the parks, rooftops, and canal side, was impressive, even on a grey and drizzly day like this, where the sun skulked low in the sky, lost in the haze, barely scraping the treetops.

Maureen Wimslow was waiting by her front door, smoking her e-cigarette. She was a hefty woman, with a jolly face, copper curls that had faded to silver, a coral pink hoodie, and peach tracksuit bottoms. She gave me a big say-cheese smile, as she saw me approaching.

"Tabitha is up to her old tricks, again is she?" I asked.

"I don't know how she got out the cage," Mrs Wimslow sighed. Her smile turned guilty. "When I got up, she was waiting in the kitchen, and just ducked under there..."

"I'll take a look," I promised.

"She's been... on the sugary stuff," Mrs Wimslow added, with a meaningful raise of her eyebrow.

Oh good. The world's smallest rottweiler was on an e-number high. I was going to have to consider her armed and dangerous. As we walked through the living room of the flat, to the kitchen, four other rats, all white, dumbo eared, little cuties, with sweetly twitching noses, apricot markings, and innocent expressions, watched us from the snuggle hanging in their cage.

The kitchen was small, and economical with its space. A washing machine, cooker, and a few cupboards had been crammed under the counter, with more cupboards above. There were scratching noises from behind the kickboards beneath the cupboards. I got down on my hands and knees, took the LED torch on my keychain, and glanced into the small airgap between the cupboard and the kickboard. A white snout and razor teeth lunged out to see if my fingers or torch were edible.

I whipped my hand away from Tabitha and she scurried out of view. I took another peep. The void beneath the cupboards was full of dust and spiderwebs, with the gas pipes, water pipes, and cables running along the wall. The little white and peach terror was curled up in the corner, with a single portion box of chocolate and caramel cereal. The box had been torn, squished, and flattened squeezing it through the gap, and had been chewed open. I levered the kickboard away from the sprung clips. The sudden light sent Tabitha into hiding. She dived into the cereal box, and the box went bolting past me, in a flurry of paws. There was a ding, as it bounced off the cage.

"Want to go catch her?" I asked.

"Oh?" Mrs Wimslow muttered, still staring at me.

"Please?" I asked. "I can check if she nibbled any wires or anything."

Mrs Wimslow smiled, and swept away. She picked up a yapping, snapping, cereal box, with a whipping tail, and dropped it into the cage, where Tabitha bounced into one of the tubes with an armful of chocolate bites.

I reached under the cupboard to inspect the cables and pipes. There was no real damage, which was a relief, as the rest of the rats had an addiction to eating power leads. Mrs Wimslow sipped her tea and told me about endless bingo players I had never met, and their complex web of secrets, lies, and fumblings in the supermarket car park. It was gossip, not confession, but even so, I think I should spare you the gory details.

Satisfied there was nothing to worry about, I snapped the kick board back in place, and dragged myself to my feet.

I was rewarded with a cup of tea and a slice of coffee cake, so good it made me tingle.

"Did you make this?" I asked, suspiciously. "Have you been holding out on me?"

"My niece made it," Mrs Wimslow said, aglow with pride. "She has a shop on the high street now. I popped by to prime the pump and spread the word."

"So, if you turn up to Bible study with a box of red velvets, I will know you have an ulterior motive?" I asked.

She giggled. "I will."

I finished my slice of cake. "Which shop on the high street?"

Mrs Wimslow wriggled her eyebrows at me. "You know... she's single too."

I flushed. "Pardon?"

"I'm just... letting you know," Mrs Wimslow said, defensively.

I thought it best not to offer any more comment.

*

The morning was still bleak and grey as I left the Cinderoak tower and made my way through the town to St Mildred's, the parish church where I act as the Curate. It was a stout, squat building of dark grey stone, set in a crowded graveyard, with a boundary wall crowned with wrought iron, and ash trees full of birds. An attempt to burn the church down, about twenty years ago, had left it a hollow shell, that had been rebuilt. I rummaged in my satchel for my keys and let myself in through the new glass outer doors, to the foyer with the community notice board, and a rack full of leaflets. The refurbishment had left the floor of the church as an open space, with seating that could be arranged as needed, for services, coffee mornings, study groups, community events, playgroups, and multi-faith events (our neighbours at the other end of the high street were using our space, three times a week, while their mosque underwent much needed repairs, and other Christian communities had a regular spot in the church between Sunday services) and pretty much anything else. Mostly it had a very modern feel, but those original features that had been preserved, firmly rooted the church in its past.

I turned on the lights, and set the air conditioner to something comfortable, topped up the water in the vases of flowers, and ensured the charity box was available for donations, before I got around to putting the kettle on. The Vicar, Reverend Marcus Troughton, was at a venerable age now, and always felt the cold. A pot of tea tended to help him settle into the hours of toil he spent making each and every sermon or school assembly perfect. Troughton was a theatrical soul, and he liked to concentrate his efforts on the colourful pomp and ceremony of the job.

Most of his other duties, the chaplainships, outreaches, charities, and the like tended to fall onto my plate, so he was only carrying the burdens he could manage.

The creak of the door, and boots on the stone floor, shook me from my thoughts. I filled the pot and left it to marinade under a cosy. I put it on a tray and went to greet Troughton, expecting to see him, wrapped in his heavy coat and thick scarf, his hat pulled down over his ears. He wasn't there.

A big, burly, barrel chested man, with a face like boiled gammon, and a shaven scalp, in a grubby tee shirt, and combat trousers, under a donkey jacket. He dragged himself around like he was carrying a weight of chains on his shoulders, and his vein was bulging on his throat.

He looked at me, his eyes narrowing. "Are you Will?"

"No. Sorry." I offered him my hand. "My name is Barley, I am the Curate here. Can I help you?"

"You can get Will out here," the burly man said, his patience frayed to tatters.

"I'm sorry," I said evenly, "the Reverend is Marcus Troughton, and other than Miss Bixby, the clerical assistant, we don't actually have a..." Something occurred to me. "Do you mean a Will somebody, or a somebody Wills?"

"Oh. I see." A meaty digit was waved under my nose. "Very clever. You think because I don't know what you look like, I won't know it's you, and you can just lie?" He shoved me at one of the pillars. "Yeah. Real clever Will. Of course, I'm stupid enough to fall for that."

"Now, hang on- " I warned him.

The fist hit me like a wrecking ball, right in my gut. The Gammon threw his whole weight behind his shoulder and slammed me into the pillar. My head bounced off the stone and scattered my thoughts. My legs went to jelly, and I dropped to the floor like a sack of coal. The gammon took a step back, so he could get a better swing on his kick. The impact sent me riding away on a wave of nausea. The world went out of focus, and my body slipped from my grip.

Somewhere, a million miles away, it curled up against the rain of kicks that cracked and crunched against my ribs.

# TWO

Bob, my twin sister, sat at the foot of my hospital bed, in the Accident and Emergency ward, and winced in sympathy for the pattern of bruises I had been left with. Like me she had hair that tended to wild curls if left unchecked, that could not decide if it was red, blonde, or brown. She shared my grey eyes, and freckles. She was missing the livid scar around the left-hand side of her throat. Somehow, everything that made me gawky and awkward, made her look willowy and ethereal. She was as beautiful as I... well... wasn't.

Today she was in her jet-black Police uniform, with a high-vis tactical vest, and sergeant stripes.

A doctor stepped around the curtain and checked my charts. "The good news is that nothing got broken. The bruises are going to be very painful for quite a while, and I'm going to sign you off from work for a little while, but... the head injuries worry me. I want to move you onto a ward, overnight, and keep you under observation, just to make sure your head clears, and there's nothing to worry too much about."

Bob nodded. I nodded too, which was a mistake.

"He's going to be okay?" Bob asked. "I mean, should I be scared, or..."

"The pain killers I'm going prescribe will be a little strong," the Doctor said, with a grin. "He might feel a little fuzzy, and closer to God for a while."

Bob flashed me smile and sat with me until I was moved to the ward.

"We'll find him," she promised. "He went into your church, he was on the CCTV, we will find him, and he will be bang to bloody rights."

"I know." I squeezed her hand. "Can somebody swing by the church this afternoon? The youth group is there, and… if he went back…"

She lifted my hand to her cheek. "Sure. I have to go. I'll be back. I promise."

"Bob, tonight," I said.

She nodded. "I'll make sure somebody goes to the Youth Group."

Bob turned to leave. She paused.

"Bobbie," I whispered. "He was looking for somebody else."

"You said Will," she agreed.

"Which means a Will, or a Bill, or somebody is going to have some bad news headed their way," I said, "if this thug works out, I wasn't… whoever he was looking for."

"I know." Bob sat back on my bed. "Let me worry about them. You worry about you, right now, okay?"

*

The next morning, I was delivered home. Bob got me settled and arranged delivery of groceries when she could be there. She helped me take the first round of my pain killers, set a reminder for the next on my phone, and left me laying on the sofa.

Marcus came by and sat with me for a long time. We talked. He closed his eyes a few times, which usually means he is praying. He was a noble, austere, looking man, with a sloping brow, a beaked nose, and a shock of white hair. His eyes had a youthful quality, but that day they were heavy with guilt.

"You didn't do this," I whispered.

He snorted a laugh. "One day you will have to tell me how you look into my head like that."

"You were a little late," I said. "You think if you had got to the church when I got there, if there were two of us, history might have taken a different path. Don't. I am glad you weren't there. I would not like to have to live with our positions being reversed."

He took a notebook from his pocket. "Right, I think I have most your projects under control, but I know a few of the regulars call you. Anybody I should be wary of?"

"Maureen Wimslow and her rats."

"Ah." He shuddered. "They look so innocent, but they know what they are doing."

"On the plus side," I said, softly, "she is determined to look after her niece, and support the budding cake shop."

Marcus brightened up. "Ah! The delightful Delia! Yes! She moved back here and is wonderful. Have you met her?"

"Only her coffee cake."

"Oh, you should!" He tapped his lips. "You know, I think she's single?"

"Maureen said that too."

"Ah." He laughed. "Did she happen to mention if Delia is impressed by older men?"

There was a clattering of feet out in the hall. The Trouble coming home from school.

I winced through the pain as I rose to my feet. Marcus grabbed at my wrist. He gave me a worried look.

"I'm okay, I have to catch my neighbour," I said, hobbling for the door, nursing my side. I made it to my door, before Helen closed hers. "Hey!"

Helen stopped and turned around, grinning with her big bright smile. "Hey!"

Her smile froze, as her eyes widened. "Oh! Barley! What happened?"

"There was a guy…" I said, lamely. "At the church. He…"

"No!" She shook her head. "Oh, no! Are you okay?"

"I'm home from hospital, but I'm on meds, and…" I waved a hand over my head. "The pain killers are working, but I'm not sure I should…erm… on Friday…"

Helen stepped away from her door. Daisy and Rose, her two kids, watched from just in her flat. Helen waved at them to shoo away.

"It's fine," Helen said. "I can get another sitter."

"That isn't fair!" Rose squeaked.

"We wanted to mess with the Dork!" Daisy agreed.

Helen looked me up and down. "Can we talk later? Did you want to pop across for a coffee?"

I nodded. "Sure."

She kissed my cheek. "Good. Sorry. I have…"

"Mum!" One of the Trouble wailed from in the house, as they scampered off. "Mum!"

"Sorry!" Helen said, flashing me that smile again, as she backed away, and closed the door.

I slouched around and waddled back to my flat. Marcus was nursing the last of his tea.

"So!" He declared. "Any tips on rat wrangling? Heavy gloves? A taser?"

"They aren't that bad," I promised him. "Just make sure they haven't left a fire hazard under the oven or something."

He adopted a thoughtful frown, that remained on his face until he went on his merry way.

I lay on the sofa for the rest of the afternoon, in the hazy bliss of painkillers, watching the antiques quiz, and trying not to wonder who the man with fists like cinderblocks, had thought I was.

That evening, after the kids were in bed, and my groceries stowed away, Bob and I slipped across the hall for a coffee. Bob sat perched on the armchair, and Helen slumped on the sofa with me, her feet on my lap so I could massage them. She melted back into the cushions, as I soothed the knots in her feet, the tension ebbing out of her as her shoulders relaxed.

"Who did he think you were?" Helen asked.

"A Will, or a Bill," I explained. "Who he thought that was, I don't know. He seemed to think I should know who he was."

"We have his pictures from the CCTV," Bob said, showing Helen the image on her phone, "but it isn't a face I know. We are making enquiries, it will be in the news."

Helen closed her eyes. "They know each other, but not in person? Is this an internet thing? Or a fantasy football thing?"

"Then why the church?" I asked.

"I have no idea," Helen confessed. "I was just thinking out loud."

Bob perked up. "Somebody drove by this evening, but there was no sign of this guy. Just some other bloke hanging at the gate, waiting on his date. He wasn't a Will either."

"Speaking of the dates," I said brightly. "Do we get to know about yours, Helen?"

"Ah!" Helen chuckled. "Her name is Peri. She's a nurse, from Australia, and has a wicked sense of humour. She also happens to be heart flutteringly beautiful, which helps."

"I hope," Bob said, cautiously, "that you are meeting her in a public place, and staying safe?"

"We did," Helen confessed. "On the first date, we met in a pub, then went for coffee, and... she is yummy. This time she's picking me up from here." She opened one eye. "I'm planning to wear the come-hither-heels, which will be painful, but worth it."

Bob snorted a laugh. "Good job you know a guy."

"Mm." Helen sighed. "Yeah, it's a shame the baby sitter is out of commission."

"Well," Bob laughed, "that was as subtle as an anvil."

"Pretty please?" Helen asked. "With butterflies and buttercups?"

"Sure." Bob sipped her coffee. "I'm already baby sitting one big kid, another two will be fine."

"They won't be trouble," Helen said, hopefully, wriggling the toes on her other foot.

I switched to that foot. "Is this okay?"

"You have no idea..." Helen said, contented. "When somebody drags you kicking and screaming into the modern age, and signs you up to a dating app, this needs to be on your profile."

Her eyes opened.

She glanced at Bob, and for a moment they were both sharing the same smile.

"No!" I said.

"No?" Helen asked, fluttering her eyelashes at me. "But… it would be fun."

Bob pouted. "We would say nice things about you, to meet nice, friendly, lovely people."

"No!" I insisted.

Helen and Bob were still grinning.

# THREE

On Friday Helen came to mine after the school run. She was nervous about the date and needed something to do other than worry about which outfit to wear. I made coffee, and got as comfy as I could on the sofa, nursing my bruises, while we played on my tablet to sign me up for her dating app. She flicked through my photographs, and found one of me in a dog collar, that did not look shambolic or too like a scarecrow.

Helen paused a moment. "Griffin, are you ready for this?"

"It's been a few years," I said. "I should…"

Helen took my hand and put it to her cheek. "Whatever happens, it won't make what you felt for Verona go away or mean any less. If she is watching, she would want you to be happy. She would want you to move on."

"Oh?" There was no anger in my voice. There's a cold slither in my heart that was surprised there was no anger. It felt very much like I should have been angry. "You didn't know her. Which is annoying, because you are right."

"Are you ready?" she asked.

I nodded.

Satisfied, Helen filled in my details, with a flurry of thumbs.

"You need a Hook," she said.

"A what?"

"Like a name, but not your name. If you called yourself Griffin Barley, any old weirdo could find you, and… well… there aren't too many Griffins in the census, are there? So, you want to be a More Tea Vicar, or something cute and funny, but not a Dog Collar, that has another connotation."

"I can imagine." I shrugged. "Does Harvest Mouse suggest anything? It was a nickname at school."

"I… don't think so." Helen grinned. "If you get any kinky messages because of it, let me know!" She showed me how to move around the app and see those who were advertising in our corner of London. "Right, this is where it gets interesting. There are sort of clues and nods people give each other, without scaring people away who aren't looking for… something special. For example… these people who are showing off more than watch? They say 'single' on their profile, but they are in open relationships. These ones making this hand gesture, are… well, they would say they were old fashioned, or…"

"Unapologetically un-PC?" I asked.

"Yes." She pointed to a woman whose face was not visible, but wore high heels, and an ankle charm. "She has a thing about her feet being worshipped. She would… appreciate your foot rub."

"Or she could just think the charm is pretty?"

"Maybe," Helen agreed. "They are a long way from universal, but stick them on your profile page, or the cover of a romance, and people will know what they are getting."

She flicked through and stopped to snort at one of the profiles. "Pah! Somebody is lying about her age! There is no way this one is in the range I set on the search options. She looks like she has a bus pass!"

"Be careful what you say," I chided her, playfully, "Maureen Wimslow, although certainly bolder and older than my tastes, is a lovely old dear, and one of my flock. No! Don't click on it!"

"Maureen," Helen said, in a sing song voice, "is apparently looking for casual encounters with adventurous young men, who appreciate her experience."

"I am quite sure I didn't need to know that." I held up my hands. "I just want to be happy she might meet the right somebody, without knowing the details of her love life."

"Or lust life?" Helen flicked past. "Want me to show you how to send them a message?"

"I can work it out," I promised.

"Well?" Helen passed me the tablet. "Go on then?"

I shot her a look. "I think I can do this bit on my own."

Helen raised an eyebrow. "Do you now?"

"Yes," I groaned.

She pecked my cheek. "Just know that if they break your heart, I will have words to say about it! I will!"

She left me with one of her smiles.

*

I spent most the rest of the afternoon listening to music, and butterflying between failing to impress anybody on the dating app, and some of the church's growing pile of paperwork. Bob poked her head in the door, on her way to babysit the Trouble. She was in her second-best blouse, her favourite jeans, and her cheekiest grin.

"Hey!" she cocked her head. "Are you okay?"

I nodded and showed her the paperwork. "I am having a wild party night."

"So, I see!" She pointed a finger gun at me. "Don't make me ask!"

"What?" I stared at her. "I've been on the app a few hours. Nobody has thrown themselves at me yet. I haven't even chatted to anybody, let alone chatted anybody up."

"Okay!" she giggled. "You know… I could watch your profile."

"What?" I scowled at her. "That doesn't sound right."

"No. Or, strictly speaking, legal, but there are ways and means, and I worry for my little brother." She pouted. "It came up in a case a couple of weeks back, and it's not as difficult as you would like to believe."

"Joy of joys!" I sighed. "Don't you dare even think about it."

My sister chuckled and rolled her eyes. "Fair enough. I better… you know…"

"Sure." I grinned. "Good luck."

She stopped. "Oh, should I worry that your boss rang me? The most Reverend Marcus wanted to borrow my CS gas and taser, so... the rats couldn't gang up on him. I think he wants you to heal quick little brother."

Little brother? By seven and a half minutes. She was sprung loaded, and I wanted a lay in.

"I'm sure he doesn't have to worry, that's just Tabitha," I said.

Bob grinned. "Awesome. Anyway, I'm off to raid Helen's wine rack, and watch cartoons. Knock on the door if you get lonely!"

Three minutes after she closed the front door, the doorbell rang.

I shuffled over to the door and opened it on the chain. A woman with a box of cupcakes and a shy, nervous, smile stared into my eyes. She was perfectly pear shaped, with sensuous curves, rosy cheeks, dyed blue hair, and peacock blue eyes. Tattoos burst out of the collar and sleeves of her polo shirt and covered the bare skin of her legs between the bottom of her skirt, and the top of her boots.

She was incredibly beautiful, just as Helen had promised.

"Oh!" she said, biting a full lip. "You aren't what I expected."

"Ah!" I ran my fingers through my hair. "Were you looking for a date?"

The woman scowled at me. "I beg your pardon?"

"Ah. No. Okay…" White hot panic, and ice-cold dread thundered around my veins, chasing each other. I swallowed. "Sorry, it's just my neighbour is expecting somebody, and she's thirteen C, and I'm thirteen B, and you have no idea how often I get her deliveries, dates, and… stuff, just knocking on my door."

Her gaze remained fixed on my eyes, staring into me, even as her expression opened from confusion to bemusement.

"I'm not… I don't leer out of my door and ask every stranger for a date!" I promised. "And for some reason I said that out loud, and now I'm pretty sure I've forgotten how to talk."

The door across the hall opened.

Helen, Bob, and two kids were watching me.

"So…" The woman held up the box. "Is there a Reverend Barley at home?"

Bob burst into laughter. "Yes, but you really should ignore my brother, he can't help being an utter spanner, but he is harmless."

"I have cakes," the woman said, holding up the box of cakes.

I opened the door and took the box from her. There was a card on the box: To Rev. Barley. Best wishes, and get well soon, from Maureen, and all at St. Mildred's."

"Ah." I could feel my cheeks flushing like beacons. "Would you be Delia?"

"Yes." Delia laughed. "And you are the one she kept telling about me being single?"

My heart jolted in my chest. I felt the pang of guilt, before I realised it was for everything that laugh stirred in my chest. Everything I was feeling for somebody who wasn't Verona.

"It's not why I... I didn't... I..." I gave up floundering and leant against the door. "Sorry. I'm just going to stop talking now."

Delia nodded. "I think that is for the best." She pushed the box of cakes into my hands.

I took the cakes in numb fingers. "Sorry."

Delia smiled, and waved a hand as though dismissing my worries. "Don't worry about it. No offence was taken." She cocked her head. "Enjoy the cakes."


"Yes." I nodded and stepped back inside. "Yes. Sorry. Bye..."

She walked off, without another word. At the stairs, she looked back, a bemused smile on her lips. She stared right into my eyes, and broke into a grin, as she hurried on her way.

Helen chuckled. "Well, that was impressive."

"Yep." Bob held up a finger, with an air of authority. "Little brother likes her."

"What?" I stared at Bob, aghast. "I don't know her."

"No," Rose giggled. "But you want to!"

"Of course, he does," Helen agreed. "That was babbling. She gave him the Babbles!"

"So, what if she did?" I groaned. "She's never going to speak to me again."

Bob grinned. "Isn't it meant to be your job to be on good terms with somebody who can help?"

I gave her a warning look, that just made the gaggle laugh louder. I flicked open the box. Six chocolate cupcakes, with mountains of velvet smooth icing, sat in their tray, smelling as good as they looked. Rose, Daisy, and Bob crowded around for a look.

Daisy turned on her puppy dog eyes. "Muuuuuuuuum?"

Helen nodded, slightly.

"Go on then," I said, helping them take one each.

Bob leant close. "Hey… You know she looked worth a Babble, right?"

I nodded.

"Attaboy!" my sister chuckled, nabbing a cake. "Right, kids, it's time we were rooted to a sofa in the company of a good film, so… what are we watching?"

As they hurried back in Helen's flat, an elfin, sultry, woman in dark jeans and a dark sweater came up the stairs. Helen transformed as soon as they saw each other, melting into a joyous smile, and a glow behind her eyes.

I made myself scarce.

# FOUR

Boredom had driven me stir crazy days before my bruises had faded enough for me to venture back into my life. Marcus said all the right things, and showed me all the right concerns, but the first time I walked into the church, in time to help out with the Senior Club coffee morning, he couldn't disguise the relief that made him light on his toes.

Mrs Wimslow was in a good mood. She literally danced over to the table with the urn, for her coffee, her eyes bright and wide.

"You look happy!" I said.

"I am!" she declared. I don't know if anybody has ever managed to look sexy and seductive as they dunked a custard cream into a white coffee, but Maureen Wimslow gave it a good try. "I have met somebody."

"You have?" I asked.

"She has," Marcus agreed. "A nice man from the internet."

Mrs Wimslow winked at me and rolled her eyes. "Well, I had to meet a lot of somebodies, but now I met the right somebody, and I cashing in those river cruise tickets with him. We have two weeks in a luxury cabin, and... I'm not planning to let him out to see the scenery."

I looked at Marcus. He looked as uncomfortable as I felt. I cleared my throat. "I'm not sure I needed quite so much detail, but... I am glad you are happy."

"Me too." Mrs Wimslow winked again. "Harvest Mouse."

I flushed. "Ah. So… the app worked for you?"

"It worked a treat," Mrs Wimslow said, with a giggle. "And you can stop looking like you sucked a lemon Teatime Reader, I am sure you will meet a new friend for cosy conversations soon enough."

Marcus swallowed. "She made the account for me."

"So…" I cleared my throat. "Who is the lucky guy?"

"Liam," Mrs Wimslow said. "He's picking me up after. Oh, and my Delia is looking after the rats? I gave her your number, just in case Tabitha gets up to her tricks?"

I nodded. "I would be very happy to help, if… she can bring herself to ask. I'm afraid I might not have made the best impression."

Mrs Winslow laughed. "She did ask how strong your painkillers were. She understands."

"And she is very nice," Marcus added, just loud enough to ensure that all the over silver haired ladies and gents looked up from their teas and coffees.

"And single?" I asked.

The pair giggled.

Something stirred in my mind, as little drips and drops of things people had said started bouncing off each other in interesting ways.

"Maureen," I said, quietly, "what's Liam's alias online?"

"Checking up on him?" she asked.

I shook my head. "It's important. Please?"

"Will I Be Yours," Maureen said. "Six Nine."

Marcus started to chuckle, but caught himself, as he tuned into my frequency. He took his phone from his pocket and tapped open an image. "I don't suppose one of the other men you met was this guy?"

"Him?" Mrs Wimslow frowned. "His name was Chris, and I had to block him. We met once, and he was... a very troubled man. I don't like bad boys like him. Why do you have his picture?"

"Would you mind telling a nice police officer about him?" I asked.

*

His name was Chris, but Maureen Wimslow knew him as Say It As I See It 336. Just as she said, she had met him once. It wasn't a good meeting, it was a date that made her call it off, and when he kept pestering her for reasons why, and complaining he deserved better she blocked him, and changed the places she met dates.

Unfortunately, with a little knowledge, and the right software, you could keep too close an eye on somebody else's account. Chris had monitored Maureen's account, but Liam had either been careful, or luckily bad at online dating. His profile picture was a landscape shot of the sea, and he had switched to a different messenger to swap pictures, phone numbers, and do the important date making, so there was very little for Chris to snoop on.

Chris had watched Maureen's flat, and when he saw somebody leaving her house early in the morning, he had deduced it was a boyfriend who had stayed the night, and not a helpful curate assisting in the capture of a wayward rat.

He followed me to the church and beat me up to warn him off 'his' woman.

*

Bob sighed and sipped her glass of wine. "They'll find him. At least Maureen and her friend are out of his reach for a while."

Helen nodded, and looked into the distance. "Does it ever work, do you think?"

We were celebrating the weekend at mine, with hand made pasta, in a sweet and spicy vegetable sauce, with chunks of a crusty loaf fresh from the oven. I was at the table with Marcus, Helen, and Bob, while the Trouble were settled on my sofa, watching cartoons, and giggling to each other.

We were trying not to talk about Peri. Things had gone well for a few dates, but the momentum had been lost, the glow had faded, and the spark fizzled out. There wasn't really a reason why, it just didn't work out as they got to know each other, and the early rush of adrenaline had waned. Helen was doing okay, all things considered.

Helen swirled the wine in her glass. "Beating somebody up, I mean, to impress the man, or woman, you thought you had dibs on? I mean, even on the worst of my dates, I can't ever imagine being impressed by somebody swaggering over, and beating the living Hell out of the girl I was trying to talk to, you know?"

Bob checked the kids weren't paying attention. "What if I worded it differently," she said, in a low, serious, tone, "and said come with me, or I don't stop here. Or, come with me, or you get hurt next? I don't think it was about winning her heart, it was about...control."

Marcus waved his fork, his gaze losing focus a moment. "My father once wrote: There is no crueller lie, than devotion demanded, not earned, through the fear of the whip, or pretending there is some mercy in staying a hand you need never have raised. There is no more haunting vision, than the hollow eyes, and tremble of fear, behind a forced smile."

Bob looked at me. Her eyes grew heavy with sympathy. "They will find him. They have his name, and his picture, and a phone number. They know who he is, and the net is out there."

I did my best to smile. "I know."

She put a hand on my shoulder. "Tell me you are okay?"

I nodded.

Bob smiled and kissed my cheek. "Good lad."

My phone buzzed on the side, dancing across the counter, displaying a number I didn't recognise.

My friends all stared at me.

I scooped up the phone and tapped to accept the call. "Hello?"

"Hello?" Delia whimpered. "Hi. So... er... Maureen said if I had rat problems you were the man to call?"

"Is something wrong?" I asked, gently. "What's happened?"

"I was feeding them, and one of them tried to bite me, and…"

"Are you hurt?"

"No." She drew the word out, her tone wavering reluctantly. "But it got away, and now it's inside the kitchen, and I can't reach it, and… it has really sharp teeth."

"It's okay," I assured her. "That's probably just Tabitha. I'll come and give you a hand, and she will be fine."

Delia drew a breath. "Right, so, do you have chain mail gloves or something?"

"Not exactly," I said, ripping a hunk off the bread. "I'll be there soon."

Marcus chuckled. "Tabitha?"

I nodded.

Marcus looked at Bob, pleadingly. "Lend him your taser?"

"No," she said, bluntly. "You go and give it an exorcism!"

"No fear!" Marcus spluttered.

I stood up and squared my shoulders. "I'll go and take care of the Mouse Of The Baskervilles, if one of you lot does the washing up."

"Not it!" Rose and Daisy shouted in unison.

"Not it!" Helen declared.

"Bugger!" Bob groaned.

*

At night the car parks, and lawns around Cinderoak tower, were well lit by lamp posts, that cast back the shadows with sterile, cold, light. Something itched at the back of my head, a feeling of being watched. I paused and looked around, scanning the velvet dark shadows, echoes of pain searing on my ribs.

All was still.

I stared into the shadows, but could see no signs of movement, of anybody else.

I hurried to the relative safety of the foyer, and into the elevator. Everything was still and empty as the doors hissed closed, and the lift whirred on its way skywards.

Delia peered out at me from behind Mrs Wimslow's front door. She smiled, and opened the door to let me in. "Oh! It is you!"

"Sorry," I said.

Her smile flickered, and my heart stuttered. "You look better. Are you back in the world of the living now?"

"I am," I assured her. "Shall we?"

Delia allowed me past, and I ducked into the kitchen. The snout and teeth of Tabitha the rat poked out from under the cupboard, as she seethed and clawed at the kickboard. I took the bread from my pocket, tore a nugget from it, and tried to tempt the rat out. It sniffed the bread, but wouldn't come out for the bread.

I tutted at the rodent. "Just once you could make this easy, you know."

"She knows who's the boss, doesn't she," Delia said, with a chuckle.

I looked back over my shoulder. "Whose side are you on?"

Delia answered with a wry smile. She was wearing a hoodie over a low-cut top that showed off her tattoos, and a pair of jeans, with heeled boots. Her hair was a dark purple, streaked with pink. Her eyes glanced between mine, and the scar on my throat.

"She didn't do that, did she?" Delia whispered.

"No." I swallowed back the sparks of anger and bile and flashed her a smile. "They aren't so bad, when they get to know you."

Tabitha snatched the bread from my fingers and retreated back under the cupboards.

Delia cackled with laughter. "Oh! Well done!"

"Hey!" I waved a warning finger. "Which of us needed reinforcements?"

I levered the kickboard from its clips.

"Hang on!" Delia said, hopping up onto the counter, and armed herself with a rolling pin.

I lifted the board away. Tabitha grabbed her bread and hopped past me for the door. I span about and caught her, scooping her into my hands. The little rat squirmed about my hand, but couldn't bite me without losing her prize. I gently stroked her soft fur to calm her.

"See?" I asked, holding her up for Delia to see. "She's kind of cute."

"If bitey," Delia agreed. "Hey little sweetie. Are you done making me look stupid? I mean, the least you could have done was make this look difficult for him."

I took Tabitha back to the cage, and she scurried into hiding with her nugget of bread. I tore the rest up and let her sisters take them. They each found a little nook or cranny, in which to devour their treat.

As soon as I closed the cage, Delia stepped out of the kitchen.

She shifted nervously. "So, are you any good at cleaning out the cage?"

"I can do, but not tonight." I stepped back into the kitchen. "Mind if I check she didn't nibble a cable?"

"Has she done that before?" Delia asked.

"Yeah. It's why the chord on the television is so short," I said. "They chewed through it, so I had to cut it back, and fit the plug further down, and further down..."

Delia chuckled, and knelt with me to check under the cupboards. Tabitha had chewed at the chipboard backing of the cupboard, but the gouges and marks were purely cosmetic. We clipped the kickboard back in place and sat back against the cupboard.

"What about Monday?" Delia asked. "After work? In the evening?"

"Sure." I cleared my throat. "I mean, if you aren't busy?"

"Well, I'm busy cleaning out rats." She frowned. "Which, weirdly, is the closest I have come to a social life since moving to London."

"Really?"

"Yeah." She shied away from me a little. "I mean, there are people I knew from university, who I met up with, but I just sort of ended up sitting alone, watching the bags."

"Well, you have my number, if you ever want to get a coffee, or a meal, or…"

"A movie?" she asked, hopefully.

"If you wanted." I suddenly had no idea what to do with my hands. "If first impressions aren't enough to put you off?"

"Well…" She rolled her eyes. "Either you aren't doing as bad as you think, or I have a wicked sense of morbid curiosity and just want to see what happens next."

"Are you sure? I am pretty sure I'm coming across as an idiot still."

"Yeah?" She patted my knee. "There are worse things to be than an idiot. Come on, I need to get home and continue my ongoing quest to discover how bad takeaways can be."

I hopped to my feet and helped her up. She heaved her ample form from the floor and clung to my arm as we walked out onto the balcony.

The big, bald, knuckle dragging thug who had beaten me senseless loomed in our way.

"Hey Will," he snarled.

"But, I'm not-" I began to say.

"Shut it!" He shoved me back towards the flat. "Where's Maureen, and who's the fat bird?"

"Fat bird?" Delia scoffed.

Chris, the bald thug, grabbed my throat, and hurled me at the railing. I landed with a thud, that burned across my ribs. He gripped my neck and pinned me to the railing. With his other hand, he reached under his coat and produced a nasty looking kitchen knife.

"Where is she?" He demanded, his words flecked with spittle.

# FIVE

Delia froze. Her fingers curled to fists. "If you must know, Maureen is on a river cruise, on the Danube, with her boyfriend."

"Yeah?" Chris the thug looked at me. "Then who is this?"

"Her priest," I said, quietly. "You really don't need the knife."

"Bull!" He waved the knife at Delia. "Don't talk at me like I'm an idiot! I'm not an idiot! I worked it out!"

"Chris," I said, evenly, "point the knife at me."

He glared at me. "Don't tell me what to do!"

My heart thundered in my chest, but somehow my voice remained soft and even. "You don't have to threaten Delia. You can point the knife at me. I'm the only one you have to be angry at."

Chris turned red, his veins bulging. "Shut up!" He changed his grip on the knife, ready to bring it down on me. "Don't tell me what to do! Maureen is mine! You hear me? Mine! You can't steal her from me!"

I grabbed the wrist that held the knife and twisted it as hard as I could. Chris yelped in pain and let go of the knife. It tumbled down off the balcony and into the yard. He let go of my throat and swung his weight behind a serious left hook.

I know the Bible says to turn the other cheek, but instinct told me to duck. The fist sailed over my head, and Chris tottered off balance. Delia ran forwards, and with a roar of primal rage, leapt into a head butt, that shattered the thug's nose, and sent him crashing to the floor.

"Are you okay?" I asked.

"Ow." She rubbed her head. "I'm okay. You?"

"I'll live." I flipped out my phone and rang the police.

"Fat bird?" Delia asked, giving the thug a swift kick.

He answered with a sob of pain.

*

Bob waltzed into the church, with a tray of take away coffees and a box of cupcakes from Delia's shop. She managed to juggle them both and snag me in a hug all at once. Marcus watched from the chair where he was polishing the silverware, a big grin on his face.

"I have good news," Bob declared. "First of all, your bald friend has been sectioned, and is a much nicer chap when he is getting the help he had been denying himself. I have to tell you, he has done nothing to help the stigma of mental health issues since his misadventures made the local news, but... it should all work out okay."

I mulled on that a moment. "That is good news."

"The better news is..." She held up the tray of coffees. "I have lattes, and velvet caramel cupcakes." She winked at me. "They are delicious, and the woman in the shop is amazing."

"Amazing?" I asked.

"Beautiful, sweet, funny…" She wrinkled her nose. "Going out with a complete dork, but there is no accounting for taste."

"We aren't going out," I said, too quickly. "It isn't a date. We are just… getting to know each other. It's a social thing. Purely platonic."

Bob nodded. "Okay. Sure. Word to the wise though? She isn't an idiot, and I just warned her you might start babbling."

"What?" I could feel my face turning scarlet. "Why?"

"Because she's beautiful, sweet, and funny," Marcus said, without looking up from his polishing.

"But…" I rubbed my head. "Why would you do that?"

"Because," Bob said firmly, "it wouldn't hurt her to know she's worth babbling over."

"True," Marcus agreed.

"Don't encourage her!" I protested.

"Oh, I think I will," Marcus said, lightly. "It's more fun this way."

Bob was nodding in agreement, as she offered Marcus his pick of the cupcakes.

"What if she cancels?" I demanded. "Knowing I find her tongue tyingly babble worthy, is more than enough grounds to have seconds thoughts."

"Then it would be her loss," Marcus said, with a mouthful of icing.

"And what if she doesn't?" Bob asked, pointedly.

"But," I insisted, "what if she does?"

"She won't," Bob assured me, "probably. Maybe. She didn't seem unimpressed."

I turned my gaze skywards. "Are you in on this too?"

"You know," Marcus said, "she can't ignore you completely, at least not for the next week and a half. Or, rather, not unless Tabitha suddenly reforms and lives a very changed life, which seems, somewhat unlikely. She will probably be calling sooner, rather than later."

Bob was nodding in agreement. "Hey... what's the worst that can happen?"

I gave her a warning look. "That is a question I try not to ask these days. It tempts fate."

# ALL THAT REMAINS

# ONE

I hopped up the steps to the front door of the tall, blunt faced, Victorian town house, through the rain, as thunder rumbled through the ink stain clouds. Smith was the name on the top of the four doorbells. I pressed the button, and there was hornet buzz from the speaker grate on the intercom.

"Yes?" A small, barbed, voice demanded.

"Dave Smith?" I asked. "My name is Barley. I'm from St Mildred's. We spoke on the phone?"

The buzzer rang, and the latch on the door cycled. I stepped in out of the rain. The hallway was dominated by the wide staircase of polished wood, that rose up past several floors, all the way to the fifth floor, and the domed skylight, on which the rain was drumming a tattoo. I dropped the hood of my sweatshirt and hurried up the stairs.

Smith was lurking in the doorway of his cramped and cosy apartment, in a grubby tee shirt, and faded jeans. He was a young man, no more than twenty-two, with features drawn gaunt and tight, around a lopsided smile, and flattened nose. He looked me up and down, his eyes lingering on my dog collar longer than I was comfortable with.

"So," he shifted uneasily, "do I call you Father Barley, or Brother Barley, or... I don't really do churches. Sorry."

"Reverend Barley," I said, with a smile, "but most people just call me Barley. Shall we?"

He nodded and waved me into his flat. As soon as I was in, he shut the door, locked it at two dead bolts, and slipped a chain.

The first thing that hit me was the smell. The cupboard sized kitchen was buried under dirty plates, and the bin was overflowing with take out containers. There were mugs and a box of tea bags, but they were outnumbered by beer cans and bottles. The sitting room was well lived in, and the coffee table had not been cleaned in a while. A laptop sat hap-hazard on the sofa, and there were video game controllers and blue-rays stacked on the coffee table. I noticed the pile of bills, and final demands on the windowsill. Things were getting desperate in his life.

Smith stood at the window, looking out over the back garden of the house, and the canal towpath. He seemed fixated on the rain. "So… how does this work?"

I gave him a helpless shrug. "That depends on what you want. You were… not overly clear on the phone."

He looked at me, his expression cold and haunted. "There's a law about this right? I confess something, and you have to listen, and forgive me, and then I'm good with God? Or do we have to go to the church, to a booth, and make it official?"

"That's more a Catholic thing," I said softly. "In the Anglican church we confess a few different ways. In some worships, like at Eucharist, we have moments of silent, confession, in which we ask you to think on your sins, and pray for absolution. Or, by Canon Law, I can hear your confession of hidden sins, to unburden your conscience, and help you seek spiritual consolation, and I will be sworn to protect your secrets."

"You can't tell the Police?" he asked. "No matter how bad it is?"

"It is between, you, me, and God," I said, "but there are…things you need to consider."

"It makes me good with God?" he asked. "God will stop punishing me, and start listening?"

"Mister Smith," I said, gently. "In my experience God forgives us easier than we forgive ourselves. I can help you seek peace, but I can not hand it to you with a few words. The right thing is not always the easy thing. I can however promise you, that if you take this step, if you choose to trust me, I will do all I can to help you, and I will be with you, no matter how hard the journey is."

"What does that mean?" He looked at me. "That you can't tell the Police, but your advice might be for me to… to… hand myself in anyway?"

"Potentially," I said. "It depends what you confess, and… how it affects the world."

Smith rested his head on the window and stared across the canal. "But doing this, it protects me?"

It was rare, in my career, to have seen absolute terror. "Protect you from what?"

He clenched a fist so tight, his knuckles went white. "You're a priest, so… you have to believe? It's your job to believe, in God, the Devil, and… ghosts?"

I looked at him. "What are you afraid of, Mister Smith?"

"I'm not mad," he said, quickly. "I'm not mad, so this all has to be real."

"How about I put your kettle on," I said, gently, "make us some tea, and you can start at the beginning."

He nodded. "Yes."

When I returned from his kitchen, with two mugs of tea, he was sat on the sofa staring blankly into the distance, far beyond the walls of the small living room. He sipped his tea and drew a long breath before he spoke.

"It wasn't murder," he said, "before you think that. We were just kids. I was fourteen, most the others were eighteen or so. We were out one night, just doing nothing much, a few beers, hanging out, that sort of thing, and we hung out along the canal. Then this old tramp came walking by. We had seen him a few times in town, and he was... he was disgusting. He was filthy, and smelly, stinking of piss, and shit, and God knows what, in dirty old rags, and a tattered coat, pushing bundles of crap from bins in a shopping trolley. It was disgusting, old newspapers, and battered cardboard, bin bags..."

"His bed," I said.

Smith looked at me, and his contorted with anguish. "We thought it was just rubbish, it was as rotten as he was. We didn't want somebody like that around. He slept in the park sometimes, and there were kids there, yeah? Or the towpath, where people walked. Women and girls. Who would want them to bump into somebody like him?"

"And you did something to... drive him away?" I guessed.

"He stank. His rubbish stank. Somebody said he needed a bath, and it just happened. We shoved him into the canal and pitched the trolley after him." Smith stared at me, his face a masque of desperation. "It wasn't cruel. It wasn't meant to be cruel. It was a joke. We were all laughing. It was just a joke. It wasn't meant to hurt him." He sobbed, as he broke down into tears. "I wouldn't have left, with the others, if we ever thought he was going to..." He stammered. "We killed him. They found the body years later, when... when they cleared out the canal, beautified it as a nature reserve. His body was still trapped, under the trolley, and... they... the newspapers said it was an accident."

"This happened when you were fourteen?" I asked. "Winter?"

He nodded. "It was somewhere about Guy Fawkes night."

"Why confess now?"

"Because..." Smith stared at me. "I see him, at night. He watches me, from out there. I see him, on the canal, by that lock, just staring up at me."

I studied the view from the window. It was a long way to the canal, and it was between the lamp posts. I could not imagine that the figure would not be lost in shadow at night.

"I know what you are thinking," Smith said, "but... I know it's him. I can feel it is him. I can feel him staring at me. And no, he is not in my head, he is real."

"Even if he was in your head," I said, softly, "would it make him any less real? What have you done about the... events in question?"

"What could I do?" He looked at me. "I thought he had a bath, and got out the water, and as far as I knew, there was nothing to think about. When I did know? I have a job, I have a life, and…it might not be much, but what happens if I go to prison? How does that help? How does my suffering help anybody?"

I paused for a moment. "What do you know of the man who died?"

"I told you, he was a tramp," Smith said, sharply. "What more is there to know?"

"His name? How he came to be homeless?" I stirred my tea. "If he was a kind man, a gentle man, a soldier, a joker, if he had family who might have deserved to know? You keep calling him a tramp, and you make it sound that is all we need to know, all the excuse you need, for what you and your friends did, but… I don't think you believe that, at all. I think you have been close to the line yourself, and you know how easily you could have been in a dire situation."

"But…" Smith looked at me. "I confessed. I'm good with God. That means you can do something about the ghost, right?"

"I can bless the house, and bless you," I said, "but you should consider the possibility that the change needs to come from you doing the right thing. I can not tell the Police what you have told me, but you can. You know how wrong you were, how grievous your mistakes were, and I think you know that whoever the man was, whatever he lost, he deserves the truth to be known." I looked at him. "I made you a promise, and I will keep it. If you choose to do the right thing, I will see that you are treated fairly."

His face flushed with anger, and I braced myself for an argument, but he resigned himself, and his expression softened. "If I go to prison, if I set this right, will… he leaves me alone?"

I put a hand on his shoulder. "I will see you get help there, as well."

# TWO

Bob entered the interview room at Cutely Street Police Station, wearing a grim smile with her sergeant's uniform, a bundle of files in her arms. She sat down and slid the file across the desk to me.

"Four years ago, the renovation of the canal area to the nature reserve dredged up a body. A man, in his fifties, dead for some years, under water. He was recognised as a homeless man seen around the High Street, from time to time, but he was never identified, we never had a name, he was given an anonymous burial."

"A sad end to any life," I whispered.

"The DCI is talking to the Prosecution service now," Bob said, her brow furrowing. "It's early days, but I think if his statements stand up to investigation, it will earn him some leniency."

"I don't think a prison can offer him any worse punishment than he has given himself," I said, quietly. "I don't know who, or what, he saw, but he made it a ghost, and he let it haunt him."

Bob cocked her head. "You have that look in your eyes."

"What look?" I asked, absently, as I flicked through the files.

"The one where cogs are spinning so fast in your heard I can see the sparks." She touched my hand. "You think you can work out who he was, don't you?"

I nodded. "I think I have to."

There was a photo of the man as he had been in life, obtained from a CCTV image. It was fairly detailed. A man weathered and scuffed by a hard life, with weary eyes, lank hair, and a scruffy beard, in dark, shapeless clothes. I snapped a picture of the image on my phone.

"It's not him," Bob said, a little too quickly. "It isn't Dad."

"That isn't the point," I told her.

"No, Griffin," she whispered. "I checked, when they found the body. It wasn't him."

I squeezed her hand. "Hey… are you okay?"

She nodded. "Yeah, it's just he's about the right age, at the right time, the same build and height… I just… didn't want you making the same mistake of hoping."

There were no words to answer that. I squeezed her hand again.

*

Fieldmarten House was tucked away in one of those streets that had once been the desirable address for the professional classes, but had slipped down the property ladder, through shabby genteel, to just shabby. The House was detached, set back in gardens, and was now a shelter for the homeless, run by a local charity.

Caroline, the manager, showed me through to the office, and dug out some lever arch files. She gave me an apologetic half-smile. "I remember him, of course. It was terrible, the way they found him."

"I don't think he stayed here," I admitted. "He was collecting bedding."

"He was here for a while," Caroline said. "He tried, but gave up after a few nights. He had a right barney with one of my staff. He thought we were going through his stuff when he wasn't in his room. That he gave us a false name is not so unusual. People do that for all kinds of reasons. He ducked out and refused a lot of the help we tried to give him. He had chances, but they came to naught. Without the basic details, we couldn't help him." She found a page. "Aha! Here we are. Hugh Mann."

"Human?"

"Mann. Dot. Hugh. No middle name. Like the pop singer. Heard of him? Fictional date of birth. A national insurance number that doesn't even pretend to look real. We checked up on him as often as we could. Clean clothes, basics, made sure he attended the Christmas meal."

"And then he just wasn't there?"

Caroline nodded. "There were rumours."

"Rumours?" I asked.

"Somebody who had been looking for him, found him, and…" She looked at me. "What do you know?"

"Nothing I am able to share."

She shook her head. "He was nice. He had problems, and he got scared, but he was kind, and sweet, and spoke to people like he…" She looked at me. "A lot of people find it easy not to care. They find excuses for things not to be their problem, for people not to be worth caring for. He wasn't like that. He couldn't help but care, even when he didn't need to." She gave me a sad smile, her finger lingering on the page of the file for a moment. "Here we are. He was with us a week. We applied for benefits, but they couldn't go through, with his false name, and false details, we tried for a job, but there was the same problem. Oh look! I managed to get him a library card, but that doesn't seem like much does it?"

"It was something," I assured her. "Thank you."

*

Helen perked up the moment she saw me stepping into the library, out of the rain. Or perhaps it was the two gingerbread lattes I was carrying. She hopped out from behind the counter and snatched away one of the coffees before asking the dreaded question.

"What are you after?"

"Ah." I gave her a sheepish smile. "Is it that obvious?"

Helen grinned and nodded at the coffee. "Kind of?"

"I was wondering if anybody remembered an old… customer? Client? User?"

Helen laughed. "You know that sort of thing is a data protection issue?"

"I just want to know if anybody remembers him. It would have been a long time ago."

"How long ago?"

"About eight years?" I asked.

She nodded to a tall, elegant, woman, who was shuffling books back into the shelves like she was dancing. Her hair was blonde brushed with silver, her body willowy and sinewy. She saw us talking and smiled.

"Lily," Helen said with confidence, "will remember. She remembers everybody."

Lily sensed us looking and smiled at us. Helen waved her over to make the introductions.

Five minutes later the three of us were stood under the canopy, by the front door, watching the rain cascading over the square. Lilly drew heavily on a cigarette and didn't seem to notice her tears. She drew a breath. "I don't care what the library card said. His name was Harry. It was about the only true thing he ever told me. He was… a good man. A proud man. He was not a very good liar, which was a shame, as most of what came out of his mouth was lies." She looked at me. "Four years ago, when they pulled his body out of the canal, I knew. I didn't want to believe it. All the time they couldn't prove it, there was hope. I knew though."

"Why would he lie?" Helen asked.

Lily laughed. It was a strange noise. It was the nervous laugh of somebody who had no other way of processing the turmoil of her emotions. "Oh, I don't think he was on the run, or in hiding. I think he had just given up on himself and was… afraid of seeing others give up on him. He tried to stay at the shelter, he gave it a few days, but when it came to making the leap, he couldn't do it."

I understood. "It happens more than people realise. When you think your spirit is broken, when people only see the worst in you, you see it in yourself. Doubts poison… everything."

"He used to tell us such wonderful stories," Lily said. "We never minded him here. We would let him wash in the toilets, we turned a blind eye if he slept in the alley out the back. We would spot him a cup of tea, and we would try, we would always try, to get him to move on, but we didn't want to bully him into making those steps, or he might run off, and…" She looked at me. "Did he do it? Did I push too hard?"

"No," I promised, "but, I am afraid it is not my place to say what happened. The Police are looking into it."

Lily nodded. "He just wanted a chat. To feel human. We didn't mind that. He said his name was Harry. Everything else was… I got the feeling he would tell stories to pretend he was somebody worth talking to, for a while. I would have rather he told me the truth. Whatever it was."

"Lily," I said, as gently as I could. "What can you tell me about him? If you picture him now, talking to you, does anything stand out?"

"Like what?"

"An accent?" I asked.

"Oh, that's easy!" She smiled, caught in a fleeting memory. "He was from Liverpool. And… he was kind of posh. Not real posh, he wasn't born with a silver spoon, but it was like… when somebody is on TV, and they all have that same air."

I made some notes. "And, was there anything else? No matter how small or silly it sounds."

"Whisper." Lilly stared out into the rain. "So many of his stories, no matter what they were about, or how obviously they were just yarns to try and make me smile, they would always have a girl in them, much younger than him. She was called Whisper."

"Thank you," I said, quietly.

"If…" Lilly took my hand. "If he has family, somewhere out there… could you… tell me? I think… I think if they would let me, I would like to tell them about him and his stories."

"If I am at liberty to do so," I said, carefully, "I will. Would you be happy to tell me about some of his stories?"

Lily nodded. She drew on her cigarette until it crumbled to nothing, then she began to talk. When the momentum took her, she found it hard to talk, and all the stories she had been carrying for years tumbled out.

*

I spent what was left of the afternoon, and much of the evening in the office at the church, stumbling blindly through searches of the public records for signs of a Harry or a Whisper. It was clutching at straws, with no surname for Harry, and no idea if Whisper was a surname, an unusual forename (I remind you I was christened Griffin, so I have certainly heard odder) or a nickname. Or, if she was just a fiction.

Marcus was writing his sermon, listening to classical music on his phone, and when he stopped to ponder which word to type next, he would wave a finger like a conductor's baton, teasing a dramatic change of key from the strings, or drawing the woodwinds into the melody.

My phone buzzed in my pocket. I flicked it out.

There was a text message from Delia: Hey. I just found you on the Threadbare Hearts App.

I grinned and responded: My profile is pretty terrible. Sorry you had to see that.

Oh? She enquired. Want to see mine?

A link popped into the message box.

"You know," Marcus said, loudly over the music in his headphones, "a man could die parched around here!"

"Tea or coffee?" I asked.

"Well, twist my arm and make me a brew then!" he said, with a satisfied smile.

I stepped into the kitchen and studied Delia's profile as I waited on the kettle. The photograph must have been a couple of years old. She was a little heavier, and a little younger, holidaying on an exotic beach, somewhere with icing sugar sand, azure sea, and a cloudless sky. She wore a long dress, that nipped and tucked in all the right places, cut low to show off her tattoos. Her back was arched, one leg raised, her toes pointed out, a charm hanging from her ankle. She stared out of the screen, a knowing smile on her lips.

You do realise, I enquired, quite how beautiful you are?

Am I? She replied, which I read in several different ways, at once.

Yes?

Are you having any luck? On the app I mean?

On the app? No.  There was a sudden lump in my throat. Although there is this one woman, I am interested in. Unfortunately, she met me in real life, so she knows I'm an idiot. But I think we are becoming friends.

Ah! Delia replied quickly. Well, friends is a good place to start, and there is no reason it can't become more if she feels the same. Which... she might, if tomorrow night goes well.

I flushed pink and tried to work out how to answer that. Everything I typed sounded stupid, no matter how many times I deleted it and tried again.

I made the tea and walked back into the office. Marcus was looking at my notes. He was scrawling over my notes from Lily's stories in felt tip.

"These are all a bit before your time, aren't they?" he asked.

I stared at him. "Pardon?"

"Cartmel and Mann, they would have been and gone before your day, wouldn't they?" Marcus insisted. "I mean, I assume they're all from their album, and LPs, but I can only get a few of them, to be honest. The singles." He frowned at me. "Why are you trying to guess songs from the arse end of the prog rock phase?"

"Sorry, but who are Cartmel and Mann?"

"The band who wrote these stories," Marcus said. "Look, Hugh Mann and Whisper, his great love, falling in love in the forest, well that was All That Remains, the big single. This one about the haunted house, is Whispers In The Rain, and this one about the card game in Paris is Little Lost Girl. I have the album somewhere."

"Wait..." I looked at him. "Can you... do you have a picture of them?"

# THREE

Bob looked at the cover of the LP, then at the photograph from the file. She looked back to the LP I had dug out of my storage lock up in the arches, that morning.

"I don't know," she said, frowning. "Maybe?"

"Look at the eyes," I said. "The scar that tugs at his left eye, and the other on his nose."

We were in the library, the next morning, armed with coffee, and pastries. Lily looked at the LP and touched one of the two faces on the glossy sleeve. She stared at me.

"It's him," she said.

Helen stepped closer to her friend. "Are you sure?"

"I mean..." Lily snorted a laugh. "I heard of this, I saw it on TV a bit when I was young enough to go to a club, and I couldn't tell you which was which, but... one of these was my Harry."

Bob nodded. "It might be?"

"It is." Lily insisted. "Which was he, the one who could sing, or the one who could write?"

"Caroline at the shelter says the same," I told them. "He even signed into their hostel under the stage name. Hugh Mann the Human. And... there is an interesting correlation with Hugh Mann's life. Or rather Harry Pedlar. The reason there was only one album and two LPs is because one day Harry Pedlar just vanished. He went on holiday and never came back. He booked out of a cottage in Cornwall, and never made it home to Liverpool. His car was found in Essex, abandoned. He didn't have any family, they had died in a car crash, before he made it big. People thought it was the stress of a second, overdue, album, or the grief of loss, or something. He just vanished."

Lily shook her head. "He hadn't spent that long on the street."

"No," Bob said, "but that makes sense. Times were changing, as red tape caught up with modern computing. It became a lot harder to live under an alias. If something went wrong with his life, if somebody came close to the truth, he might not have been able to keep afloat, and fallen through the gaps. It makes sense of the lies too. He didn't have a dirty secret, he just couldn't be Harry Pedlar, as somebody might connect him to his fictional self."

"So, what happens now?" Lily asked.

Bob sipped her coffee. "Clifford Briggs who used to be Freeman Cartmel, before he shaved the beard and curls to go solo, is still around. I think me and Griffin can see him today."

"Oh, the troubles you go to," Helen sighed, dramatically.

"Erm..." Lily waved the LP at me. "Do you need this back right away?"

"No," Bob said, sweetly. "It's from our father's old collection. Take as much time as you need. I am sure Helen can get it back to Griffin when you are done."

I nodded.

Lily smiled. "I sort of remember the songs, but... I guess they are all going to sound different now. Knowing he's... knowing it's Harry."

"If," I pointed out, "it is Harry."

She stared at me, her gaze betraying grief and heartbreak. "It is."

*

We parked in a part of the Docklands that had been renewed and reinvented as fashionable flats with views of the city. Too fashionable for any mortgage I could afford. Bob gave me a look with a raised eyebrow as we buzzed on the door.

"How the other half live, eh?" she asked.

I nodded.

The intercom crackled. "Hello?"

The voice was dry and grizzled, like broken glass and smoke.

"Hello!" Bob said, brightly. "I'm Sergeant Robin Barley, of the Met? We spoke on the phone?"

"Third floor," the voice said, as the intercom chimed, and the door released.

We rode the lift up to the third floor, and emerged onto a landing painted white, decorated with mirrors, and potted plants. One of the front doors was open, and a bald man, with a neatly trimmed beard, and a swarthy, complexion, watched us, half in and half out of his flat. He was dressed in loose lounge clothes, all of them marked with expensive labels. He offered Bob his hand. "Hi! Clifford Briggs, and who's this? Your moral support?"

"My brother," Bob said, curtly, but kindly. "It's a little odd, but he's the one who brought us some new information. Now, this is just a possibility, and realistically we are hoping to eliminate it from our enquiries. We are trying to identify a dead body sir, and we would like to be sure it wasn't Harry Pedlar."

Briggs stroked his chin and gestured us to one of the sofas in his stark, minimalist living space, decorated with framed gold and platinum albums, those produced under his own name. He held out his hands. "No offence, but I think you are wasting your time. I've had so many podcasters, writers, citizen-journalists, coming here with theories, that I'm immune to it. Where does the padre think he's seen Harry? Doesn't really matter, does it. He doesn't want to be found."

There was something about the way he said it, about the way his smile tweaked, with easy confidence.

I cleared my throat. "You know where he is, don't you?"

Briggs nodded. "I know where he was, twelve years ago. I haven't heard from him since, but he was happy, he was at his peace, and given all he had gone through."

Bob opened the file. "Perhaps you should tell us what happened."

"In confidence," I assured him.

Clifford sighed. "There's a thing... On the scene, we have this thing. We call it getting a case of the Cuckoos. You are about to do a big show, a concert, a tv thing, whatever, and you wake up that morning, and you can't believe you are about to be there, and do that thing, then it happens. What if people realise you are just you? Not a rock God, not a composer, or a poet, just some bloke from a Council Estate, who got lucky. You think you don't belong there, that you didn't earn it, and if you aren't careful, being the person people expect you to be, playing the role, can rip you apart. It ripped Harry apart, and he gave up on it. He was happier to just go back to work, and not try. He scared us, but... eventually, after the investigation had died down, and the Police stopped I sort of... found him, and he told me what he needed. He was in a better place, and he knows I'm here if he ever needs me, but... having me turn up to see him would undo his good work and leave him fragile like. If he hasn't been to see me, I know he's okay."

Bob nodded, understanding. "Good. Then... I hope this is a quick process of elimination, and I can be sorry I put you in an... awkward position."

"No, that's fine." He looked between us. "Of course, if I ever get a sniff of this in the press, or on a podcast, and you put Harry's happiness at risk, I will see you drown in legal ramifications."

Bob passed him the file. "Would you mind telling me if you know the gentleman in these images?"

Clifford opened the file. His smile grew small and sad. "My God! What happened to him? Is he... Has he been sleeping on the streets? Is he in a shelter somewhere? Can I go... The daft bugger was meant to come to me! Can I go find him?"

Bob leant forwards. "I'm very sorry sir. The body of this man was recovered from a canal, some years ago, and was not able to be identified. We know he was homeless and had been... dead for some years before he was discovered."

Clifford wept. He looked between us. "How? How did he die?"

"Shall I make us tea?" I offered.

Clifford scowled. "New information? Did... did somebody do something to him?"

Bob chose her words carefully. "We are investigating."

"It's..." Clifford choked on the words. "It's him."

Bob nodded. "What name was he living under when you last saw him?"

Clifford told us all he knew, and we began to see how Harry ended up on the streets.

*

Bob and I sat in the car, at the riverside, watching the ducks, while Bob made a few phone calls, to the companies Harry had worked for. She thanked somebody and flicked off her phone. She glanced at me, with a slight shrug. "It was like we thought. The company he worked for changed hands, and the larger company made better checks on their staff. They noticed something screwy, which I'm guessing is a flaw in his cover identity, and he went to ground. I guess he never made his way back out of trouble."

"How do you do this?" I asked.

She shrugged. "You keep remembering it needs doing."

"No," I said. "How do you do this and not bring it home?"

"Are you seeing Delia tonight?"

"Yes," I said.

"Then," Bob smiled, "for a couple of hours nothing else will matter, because she is in your world, and she will be your world."

"So..." I cleared my throat. "You stopped telling me about that guy."

"That guy has started talking about his girlfriend, and how he talks about her makes me... considerably less envious of her." Bob chewed her lip. "You know that phase I went through?"

"Dad said it was a phase," I muttered, "I'm still pretty sure you were in love."

"Yeah." Bob smiled. "If that happened again, would it be a problem for you?"

"If you were in love?" I shook my head. "That is never going to be a problem."

"Right." Bob looked at me. "So… the App you use? Helen showed it to you, right?"

I nodded.

"And she's on there?"

I nodded again.

"And…" Bob flushed. "She's really nice, isn't she?"

"As are her kids."

"I love her kids," Bob whispered. "I love her too. It is… well on the way of being the kind you fall in. I'm asking her over to mine."

"Good."

"Just so you know." She looked at me. "You know, so you can be free, and available to baby sit."

"I will be," I promised. "Any time you need me."

She smiled. "Well, you might have your own plans."

"We can work it out," I said.

She grinned. "We can. Good."

# FOUR

I got to the restaurant too early, nervously early, so I hung out over the road, on the bridge over the canal, watching the narrow boats nested along the bank. I was in my best shirt, second best trousers, and the jacket that I only wore for dates and funerals.

Delia was walking onto the bridge from the other side. She was in a leather jacket, an embroidered blouse, black trousers, and boots with a come-hither heel that put a certain sway into her step. She leant on the bridge beside me, her supernova smile framed by hair dyed plum purple, that shone like neon.

"Hey," she said.

"You're beautiful," I spluttered, in a sudden fluster.

She stroked the tattoos on her neck, and flushed pink, smiling lost for words.

"I mean… can I try again? Hi. How are you?"

"You were doing fine the first time," she promised me.

"You look amazing."

"Oh?" She stared into my eyes. "Say the first thing again?"

My heart stopped. "You are beautiful."

"I almost believe you."

"Can I…" I waved in the general direction of the restaurant. "Do you want a drink first?"

"Fuck me yes." She giggled. "Sorry. I don't... that was not very reverential of me. I..."

"Drink?" I asked.

"A pint of real ale," she said, taking my arm. "I need it. I'm terrified."

I took her arm, and we made a beeline for the pub on the corner. She sipped her beer, and I worried over a lime and soda.

"Want to tell me about your day?" she asked.

"It isn't good dinner conversation," I warned her.

"Oh?" She put her hand on mine. "Are you okay? This isn't something where somebody could hurt you is it? No knife wielding thugs?"

"No." My heart caught in my craw. "Sorry, I'm not at liberty to tell you the details yet."

She cocked her head. "Was anybody hurt?"

"Too many people." I looked at her. "One person was harmed, years and years ago, but it never ends with one person. Hurt one person and you open a wound that festers. The pain spreads. Grief, loss, guilt, shame, infect those around us, who suffer, and their suffering spreads to those around them, and so on, radiating outwards. I started pulling a thread, and there are so many touched by the... darkness..." I looked at her. "I should stop talking, or I will suck the joy from tonight and pass the infection onwards."

"No." Delia cupped my cheek. "Don't say that. Tell me if you are okay to do tonight?"

I stared into her eyes and felt like I was teetering on the edge of an abyss. My fear melted into the background. "I want to remember there is still life beyond the calling. If you still want to see me?"

"I want to see you." She leant over and pecked my cheek. "Am I really beautiful?"

"You are... really, really, beautiful."

She chuckled. "You really believe that. I just wanted to be sure."

"Tell me about your day," I said.

"I went to meet some clients and interviewed them about a wedding order." She smiled. "They want four tiers of cupcakes with a vanilla cheesecake topping for their wedding cake, and enough other cakes to feed a very hungry reception party."

"Wow," I grinned. "Do they need a minister? A church? Somewhere for the reception?"

"No." She narrowed her eyes. "If anybody intends to get married in your place though, I trust you will tell them you swear by a very talented local baker?" Before I could answer, she shuffled closer to me, and stroked her hair back behind her ear. "You don't really want to hear about baking and icing, do you? It's my every day, my grind."

"Very well." I sipped my drink. "Ask me about anything, other than work, or subjects covered by the veil of confidentiality."

Mischief flashed in her eyes. "Anything?"

I nodded.

She stared at me for the six longest seconds I have ever experienced. "Are you a virgin?"

I shook my head.

"I mean, if you were, it would be okay," she ran her fingers on my wrist. "It's a priestly thing, right? The sanctity of the union, and saving yourself for marriage, and…"

A fair question. One that deserved an honest answer before we committed to anything, before things got… complicated. I tried to keep it matter of fact, and even handed.

"The Anglican church has not expected us to be celibate since the sixteenth century," I said. "I can date, I can be in love, and express that love. As you might imagine however, my station demands I set a certain example, and act accordingly."

"But you weren't always a priest," Delia noted, gently.

My cheeks flushed. "No, but I was before I met Verona."

"Verona?" Delia purred her name, which almost tore my heart in two. "Who is she?"

"My… We were in love,"

Delia smiled. "I have exes too. She was the big one?"

"The only one." I looked away. "We don't have to talk about her."

"Oh, yes we do!" Delia smiled. "Tell me about her. Please."

"Do you know what a curate is?" I asked.

"Like…" Delia chewed her lip. "You're the second priest in a church? The assistant priest?"

"People receive the calling at different times in life, for different reasons. When they become priests, they are stationed with a more experienced cleric, to learn all the things you can't teach. Like an apprentice? My first placement was in a village called Chestnut Bridge. The Reverend was James Othello, and his daughter was Verona, named for the city in Italy where she was conceived, where her mother was from. She was… breathtaking. She was a few years younger than me, beautiful, kind, and dedicated. She was studying maths at university. She wanted to be a teacher, but she could have been anything. She had a plan though, and she was going to be oh so very happy."

"Happy with you?" Delia asked.

"Eventually." I closed my eyes. I could still see her smile, her way of looking at me, when she didn't think I had noticed. I could smell her perfume, and feel her breath on my neck, before the scars, the breaking glass, and the blur of confusion. I could still feel her cheek turning red under the palm of my hand, on the best morning of my life. "She came home for the holidays, and we just clicked. I started looking for any spare moment I could, to drive over and see her, and she started coming home every weekend. She said it was to see her father, but we always hung out, and… as soon as I admitted what I felt for her, and she didn't laugh at me, life started rocketing past, too quickly. She was my first love, my first kiss, and…"

"And?" Delia enquired. "The reason you aren't a virgin?"

Second thoughts clouded my brain. "Sorry, I shouldn't be... We didn't date. We were best friends, and it just happened. I had a date when I fourteen, with a girl who hoped I would do her science homework, and tonight. We're not even at the date, and I'm babbling. I'm blabbing about my ex, which I'm guessing is very much wrong?"

"Tell me about her. What happened?"

"We were at the flea market, looking for something for her birthday. There was a ring, it was silver, set with art deco ceramics, not worth much, but beautiful, and she adored it, so we tried it on. It was too small for her pointing finger, but she reckoned she knew it was two sizes smaller. She put it on her ring finger to show me and couldn't get it off." I couldn't help but laugh, when I thought of that moment. I could never resist it. "I just asked what if we paid for it and left it there. Her eyes went like saucers and she told me not to be so daft, as people would think we were engaged. I nodded and asked what if we kept the ring just where it was and spent the rest of our lives together. She stared at me, and laughed, and cried, and said yes, all at the same time. That night, we... expressed everything we felt for each other, everything she had known, but I didn't have the words for, and..."

I trailed off. Delia was still smiling. She was rosy and warm, and staring into my eyes.

"Things didn't work out?" she asked.

"They didn't have a chance to," I said. "She died."

"Died?" Delia gripped my hand. "How?"

"Just before Christmas, before her house mates all went their separate ways, they threw a party. I drove out, and for the whole night, I was never further from her than our fingertips. She tried not to let go of my hand, the whole night. When the music got too loud, we lay on the picnic table, in their garden, watching the stars, our breath a silver mist, and we just talked, all night. The next morning, I drove her back to her parent's house. It was… They had this big old house, Tudor bricks and ancient oak, set deep in a farm with hop fields. The fields were all covered in fresh snow, and there were talons of ice hanging from the hop frames and the wire, the trees in the orchard, the woods… They caught the sunrise, and shone the colour of embers, like the countryside was afire."

"It sounds beautiful," Delia said.

"It should have been. I parked at the side of the house, by the trees, and we sat there, trying to bring ourselves to be apart, if only for the morning. She smiled, and said she didn't want to let me go, she wanted to stay at my fingertips. She wanted to spend the day, making up for lost time. She told me to close my eyes, like she did every time we kissed and, her lips touched mine, and… she was gone."

My heart stopped. The world stopped. Everything froze.

"There was a noise," I said, my throat dry, and my lungs grating. "It was like a whip crack, and a thud. Her lips left mine, and she grunted with pain, all in one movement, at the exact same time something hit me here..." I placed my hand on my chest. The surgical scars were faded now. There was not much left to feel of the bullet that had glanced punched through Verona, from front to back, and smacked into my chest. I could smell the blood in the air, and feel the cold fugue of shock, as I realised what had happened, as the pain caught up with her. Her lips parted, and her mouth formed an 'o'. "It had gone right through her middle. Then another crack, and..."

And Verona flinched. She fell sideways, slumping against the dashboard. There was a neat hole in her forehead, and her eyes were... missing their focus, their intelligence, the divine spark that made her a person, more than just meat, was... gone.

"She was dead," I said. "She fell away, and I saw Dad, my Dad, in the trees at the at the edge of their land. He was staring down the sights of this antique rifle, wooden stock, metal barrel, an old warhorse of a rifle. He snapped the bolt and kept firing. The next bullet should have killed me, but was a gnat's tail too far to one side." I parted my curls, so she could see the scar that ran the length of my head, behind my ear. "And again." I tilted my head, so she could see the ugly scar on my neck. "This one got infected and healed bad. I lost blood and passed out. Dad was gone. A couple of weeks later, while I was still in hospital, he took some pot shots at Bob, my twin, she... wasn't hit, thank God, but... she was the last one to ever see Dad again."

Delia sat, staring at me, her mouth open, struggling to find the words.

"Yeah," I agreed. "I am really bad at dating."

She stroked my hair away and felt my scars. "You were in love with her?"

"I was so in love with her, that for a long time, I didn't think I could live without her. Just… exist." I looked away. "My sister, my friends, my vicar, all thought I was ready to move on. I… didn't want to, for a long time, and then I thought I had to, but I never wanted to…until you."

Delia smiled. "I am glad you did."

I let out a breath. "Sorry, I sort of started talking and now…"

"I asked." Delia chewed her lip. "I asked, and you were honest."

"So…" I chewed my lip. "Can I ask?"

Delia looked at me. There was a moment of hesitation, before she nodded. "Yeah, well, asking me about my exes? That is a long… There is a lot of ground to cover, and some of it is stuff you should probably be warned about before we start. I tried getting to know people, and letting them see the real me, before they learn about… this… and it always ended up burning me when I told them. Like I was whipping off a mask, and saying 'this is who I really am', and…"

For a moment, just a moment, as she looked into my eyes, I could see all the way to her soul. I could see all the way to her guilt, shame, and the absolute terror she spent her whole life defying.

"Want to tell me over three courses and coffee?" I asked.

# FIVE

We sat in a dark corner of the restaurant, in honeyed candlelight, and velvet rich shadows.

Delia stared into her soup and didn't look at me. "I like who I am now. I like what I've made of myself. It took some work. When I was a kid, I was... lost. I didn't think I was worth anything. I wasn't doing bad at school, but I wasn't doing well, and I was fat, which meant I was bullied, and because I didn't know anything else, and because I couldn't tell the difference between feeling good about myself, and feeling... superior to somebody else... I was a bully. There were guys. Older guys. I was sixteen, and they were twenty somethings, students mostly, from good schools at good universities, from good families. The kind of good that means 'expensive'. I met them online, and we got talking, and... when we met, when I was with them, grinding them into the bedsheets, it was... For a while I was in heaven. I was wanted, loved, needed, more than anybody else. The best of them was Edwin, Eel, as his friends called him. He was... we met for a hook up, but he asked to see me again, and we had dinner, and it was about as real a relationship as either of us had ever had. I hung out with him, and we did real adult stuff. I was in Sixth form, and I was going to dinner parties, and talking about history, and art, and politics, and... getting high. Getting really high."

She looked up at me.

I put my hand on hers, and let our fingers curl together.

Delia smiled, sadly. "Ever notice how you hang out with some people, and they think the rules are different? Like… like they are acclimatized to some wrong. My Dad? He really hates speed cameras. He says they are a tax on driving normally, and that people should just be trusted to be safe. Any car that overtakes him on the motorway? Anybody who dares drive faster than him? They are dangerous menaces he screams and rages at. If a guy sleeps around, he's a lad, a hero, admired as being the most manly he can be. If a girl does it? I've been called a slut, or worse. Eel never said that though. No, with Eel, and the public-school guys, it was drugs. If I got high with them, they complained about the Police. When their friends got busted? It was the Police taking easy prey, good families who weren't hurting anybody. The Police could be out catching real criminals. I guess that's the thing. Nobody ever thinks they are a real criminal, do they? They all have excuses, or reasons, that if you saw the world through their eyes, you would understand. I was stupid enough to think I was in their group. That I was just a good person not doing any harm. If I got high with them, I was Rockstar. If I ever took some home to get high? I would have been one of those criminals they thought deserved to be ground under the heel of society." She sighed. "There was a party, and there was a boy at the party, Jeff. He was nice. He grew up on a Council estate, his parents worked hard their whole lives, he was drowning in student debt to get through University, and was always nervous, because it was this one big chance of his, to be a doctor, and he was always wound so tight, but he was cute. Eel's housemate, Sophie, adored him. She was so in love with him. He liked her too, he was just so wound up. Eel had a plan. We had a plan… I thought I could unwind him. I wasn't going to… nobody was going to take advantage, he was just going to relax a little, let his guard down, and maybe, hopefully, fingers crossed, open his heart a little." She closed her eyes. "Eel and I spiked his drink. He got high, but it freaked him out. We put him to bed and got on with the party, and when I tried to wake him the next morning, he was cold... and grey, and..." She closed her eyes. "And that was when I learned I wasn't part of the gang and didn't have friends. I was the slut sleeping with an older guy, whose friends knew me. I was shoved out from my circle of friends, and I landed in prison, and..." She waved at herself. "This, this is the person I chose to be when I got out of prison, and back on track. When I went back to college and built on the lessons I took on the inside, the tattoos, the hair, the smile, the new me. The real me. The one people like until they realise I..." She chewed her lip. "My aunt believes in me, but a lot of that is denial. She tells people I'm great, and I'm single, and she pretends I didn't kill a boy. She didn't tell you that, did she?"

I shook my head.

"She wants you to see me, to like me, then to have this conversation, and... by then, for it to be way too late, because you already like me." Delia chuckled. "It doesn't work. I get to know people, and it all goes... amazingly, until we have this conversation, then they don't know if I'm telling them that the person I've been until this point, is a lie. I think... I think that I need to rip the band aid off right away, and tell people what I was, what I did, and hope... maybe..."

"Somebody will appreciate the honesty and still give you the chance to prove who you really are, from the very start?" I asked.

She nodded.

I squeezed her hand.

At last she looked up at me, and right into my eyes.

"Okay…" She whispered. "Can we…"

"Do the date thing now?" I asked.

"Do you still want to?" she asked, freeing her hand from mine, slowly.

"Yes." I couldn't look away from her eyes. "Very much."

Her smile grew bolder. "Very much?"

I nodded.

Her smile grew again. "Okay. So… why me? Of all the girls you know, why me?"

"I…" I flushed. "I don't know. I never met a woman who made my heart change beat, like your smile makes it change, before. I loved Verona, with all my heart, but it wasn't like this. I met you, and there was this realisation that I wanted to know you better, this idea that maybe we could be something… not friends… but something, and… I don't know any other way of finding out if it was there, other than seeing you again."

She nodded. "Yeah. It's not just you. I mean… the first moment you saw me, when you asked if I was looking for a date? I was… shocked, and knocked off my foot, and it was weird, and creepy, and stupid, but the answer would have been yes."

"It would?"

She nodded. "I got out of your building, and it just hit me. And I had to stop myself running back in, to just ask…"

"What stopped you?"

"It being weird, and creepy, and stupid, and… I mentioned creepy?"

I nodded. "I can not apologise enough. In my defence, the only description Helen gave me was amazingly beautiful, so… it did fit."

"Wait." Delia leant forward. "The woman on the stairs?"

I nodded.

"Woah." Delia grinned. "Did it work out?"

"For a while."

We fell into a comfortable silence.

"So…" Delia flushed. "You want to walk me home after this?"

"Yes."

"And," she said, softly, "if I invite you in for coffee, that would be okay?" Her inflection was very careful not to make 'coffee' sound like a suggestion of anything else. "Please?"

# SIX

Poor Delia.

We spent the rest of the night talking about cartoons, books, and movies. We compared notes on the action figures we had both collected as kids and noted how many of the same TV shows we had been addicted to.

The whole time I could see her fighting the urge to ask about my Dad. It was there, behind her eyes, a melancholy note in the bonfire of joy, hope, and... longings I saw there.

I walked her home along the towpath. As we neared the lock, Delia gripped my arm. She pointed to the lock gate.

"Hello! What's that?" she said, with admirable curiosity, dragging me over for a look.

There was a framed photograph of Hugh Mann, a promotional image, that, from the watermark, had been sourced on the internet, and printed on good quality paper. There was a candle, and a note that read: "Rest in peace. You were loved, and you are missed."

Delia frowned. "I know that face. I think my mum had a Best Of album for him."

"He died here," I said, thoughtfully, "not that anybody really knows it was him yet."

And that was it. Bits of ideas aligned in my head, and everything rang true. I looked up and found myself staring at Smith's flat.

"Somebody knows," Delia said. "And they miss him."

"Yes," I agreed. "It's the ghost."

Delia beamed at me. "A ghost?"

"Not exactly, it's all a matter of how you look at it." I flashed her a sad smile. "Sorry. I was told something in confidence, and now... I understand it, I just don't know what to do."

"I know what you will do," Delia said, cupping my cheek with her hand. "You will do what is kind, and fair, and... what is right." She drew me close and pecked the cheek with a kiss, as her fingers withdrew. "So... did you still want that coffee?"

"I would love a coffee," I said, her kiss still burning my cheek. Coffee was as good excuse as any to spend time with her, and I wanted every second I could.

It scared me how much, and how easily, I wanted to spend time with her. It terrified me how easily I pushed the sense of guilt deep into my belly.

We walked to a small flat in a mid-terrace house, and Delia put a finger to her lips, as she crept down the stairs to the cellar level, to what had once been the scullery, kitchens, and servant's rooms. She eased her front door closed behind us and kicked off her boots with a sigh of obvious relief.

"Are you okay?" I asked.

"It has been a long day," she answered, on her way to the kitchen, "but worth it. Go and make yourself at home."

Her lounge was beautifully messy, with cookery books, folders full of orders and receipts, guidebooks for hygiene standards, and a swathe of comic books, novels, and DVDs. One wall was clad in shelves that bulged under the weight of her collection.

I nosed through the books, trying to get a feel for her tastes. There were horror stories, adventure yarns, romances, and many, many fantasy tales, all big, colourful, larger than life stories, escapes from the real world. There was little cork board, that held nine different book marks, and I spotted at least two more in use.

Delia walked in from the kitchen, with a couple of mugs. She put the coffees on the table and slumped onto the sofa. Her brow pinched, and her lips pursed, as she rubbed one of her feet, with a slight frown. "The boots were a mistake, but I love the way they make me look."

"Here," I said, sitting next to her on the sofa, "let me?"

Delia lifted her feet and lay them on my lap. She raised an eyebrow. "You know what you're doing, right?"

I worked the knots of tension from her feet. "There is a lady who runs evening classes at the church, and I sign up to prime the pump, so to speak, and fill out the spaces. I'm qualified in Swedish massage, aromatherapy massages, deep tissue massages, reflexology, and Chinese foot massage, and a few other techniques. If I ever want to change careers, I can dig the massage table out of my spare room."

"That's not…" Her words trailed off, as she sat back with a soft moan. "Oh, that's good."

She closed her eyes, and let out her breath, her body melting back into the sofa. Her fingers toyed with a curl of her hair.

"Is that okay?" I asked.

She lifted her other foot and put her toe to my lips. "Shh. It's fine."

I smiled, and she laughed, taking her foot away.

There were tattoos on her feet, down to her toes, of flowers and ribbons. I massaged the toes, with gentle, tender manipulations. Delia sighed again, as she muttered contentedly under her breath.

*

My alarm shook me awake too early the next morning. I lay on my bed and clung to my confused and blissful dreams as long as I could. Eventually though I surfaced to the beeping tone of my phone. I tapped the alarm off and dragged myself out of bed.

I bought some coffees on the way to the church. Marcus was waiting for me, with a broad smile.

"You look tired," he said, amiably. "Long night was it."

"You were right," I admitted. "Delia is quite wonderful."

"Only quite?" He retorted. "And you…"

"Went back to hers for coffee and conversation, after dinner," I assured him. "It was all quite chivalrous."

"Oh?" Marcus asked, a little too innocently.

I shook my head.

"Oh." Marcus put a hand on my chest. "And how did it… go?"

"Do you mean to ask if I was ready?"

"Yes," he said, warmly.

"I don't know. Yet." I held up a finger to change the subject. "Would you be able to see to things here if I went out? I have something I want to do?"

"Ordering a bunch of flowers?"

"Remember the ghost you sent me out to investigate?" I smiled. "I think it is about time she met Mister Smith."

*

Dave Smith sat at the table in the visiting room of the prison where he was held on remand. He was looking tired, and sad, his shoulders slouched, his eyes lined by restless sleep.

"Reverend Barley," he said, as she sat. "Who is this?"

Beside me Lily sat rigid and taut. Her expression was one of a woman struggling to contain her fury.

"This," I said gently, "is Lily. She works at the library, and she was good friends with an unfortunate man called Harry Pedlar, a man I want her to tell you about?"

"The tramp?" Dave asked.

"No!" Lily seethed. "The poor man, the kind man, who… did not deserve to die alone, terrified."

"It wasn't like that," Dave insisted.

I put my hand on Lily's. "Lily, I want you tell Dave about the walks you take every night."

Lilly nodded. Her body remained taut, but her voice softened. "Years ago, when they pulled the body from the canal, I began... walking to the lock. I tried to believe I did not know for sure, but deep down, I did. So, I went to where he was found. I stood, there, a little while, every night, to make sure somebody remembered, somebody mourned him. I didn't have a name, or a grave to place flowers on, but it was quiet, and it was like... the separation was thin there. In the peace, in the quiet, I can almost feel his presence. I can almost hear his voice."

"By the lock?" Dave repeated.

Lily nodded. "Now I have a name, and I know more of his life, and... his songs, his stories, were so much more beautiful than anybody ever guessed. Make no mistake, even as I knew him, at his lowest point, he was... he was wonderful."

Dave nodded. "I just thought..."

"He was nothing?" Lily asked. "He wasn't worth a second thought?"

"I know." Dave bowed his head forwards. "Would you mind... would you tell me about him?"

Lily did. She told him all the stories, all the jokes, all the times Harry found a word to make her smile.

All the times she had tried to help, and he had refused.

Dave, to his credit listened.

I sat there and tried not to think of those last few terrible moments of Harry's. Of the shock of cold water stealing his cries as a gasp, and making his struggles fade too quickly, until his limbs were leaden, his fingers numb, unable to grip the side of the canal, to pull himself out. The rush of adrenaline, the pounding of his heart, in those last moments, when he knew he couldn't hold on, or fight the weight of his soaking clothes, that he would slip beneath the surface, and down into those last, desperate, thrashing, clawing, seconds.

And then?

The merciful embrace of the God I loved, or the oblivion of my doubts?

I placed my hand on Lily's, and she looked at me. She smiled a moment, a thin, lonely, smile, hopeful and kindly.

"I can't forgive you, yet," Lily said. "I'm sorry. I try, but… I want to, one day, when I can. It's what Harry wants, up there, where he belongs. Where he has his peace. He would… he would want me to forgive you."

It wasn't a happy ending. Happy endings take far too long to find. It was, however, a start of one, and some days, that is more than you can dare hope for.

# WHERE ANGELS FEAR

# PROLOGUE

How do I even begin to explain?

First you have to understand that my father was not an evil man. He was one of the best, truest men I ever knew. There was not a time he was not a time that he was not kind, patient, caring, dutiful or sweet, or that he could not find a moment for his children, or his family. Especially his sister. He adored her.

Mum left us when we were young. I never knew her. It was always Dad, Aunt Flo, and us kids.

You have to understand my father was a good man, or you will never understand the full evil of his actions.

*

Maybe I should start here:

The last time I saw my aunt Flo was a rainy Tuesday. I was a student, residing at a theological college, at the time. On the first weekend I had free, I drove back to London. Not home. To her room in the hospital. It was a private room, in a specialist unit, looking out over grey rooftops and colourless streets.

It was Flo's fault I became a priest. I took her to church, I helped her when she volunteered, and she got me volunteering too.

There was little left, of the woman I loved. A pale, skeletal, drawn woman, gaunt before her years, lay on a bed, rasping through an oxygen mask. She tried to smile, as I sat with her, and read to her, but it was weak, failing, try.

I spent what was left of Friday, and most of Saturday, standing vigil over her.

"You should go," she whispered, on Saturday evening in one of her more lucid moments. "You don't want to see me like this."

"I don't want to," I answered. "I want to be here for you, as long as I can."

"You've been here for me," she mumbled. "And I know you love me. You don't have to do this. You don't have to see me like this. Go."

"Is that what you want?" I asked.

"What I want?" She gripped my hand and looked up at me. "What I want is to be without this... poison in my blood." She shook her head. "What I want is to not be eaten from the inside out." Something behind her eyes hardened. "You... you don't want to hear what I really want. What I beg the Lord for."

Her tone terrified me. "Hey. They are cutting the tumour out in a few days, and you are going to be back better than before. You are going to have a long life left to live."

"With an immune system shot to pieces?" she whispered. "With my body rotting from the inside out?" She squeezed my hand. "I will survive this. I don't think that means I get to do much living."

I shook my head. "Then tell me how to help you live."

"Oh, Griffin, you are going to be a good little vicar," she whispered, touching my cheek. "You can't help me. It ain't in your heart to do what I need. Just see my soul safe, eh?"

There was a knock at the door.

Dad loomed in. "Are you two conspiring?"

"Hey," I said.

"Griff, you can go," Dad said, with a smile as cold as a shark. "Flo's right. You can't burn yourself out here. Go and rest and go back to your studies. I have this."

I stepped out of the room and closed the door. A nurse smiled at me.

"What were you telling him?" Dad demanded.

"Nothing," Flo groaned. "I just… he's a good listener. He understands. He tries to keep me holding on."

Dad did not sound like he believed her.

The operation was mostly a success. The majority of cancerous tissues were removed, and although it had spread, Bob said the doctors were cautiously optimistic about treatments for the rest. We never got the chance to find out. One night, before I could head back and see her again, Flo passed peacefully in her sleep.

Dad was broken by the news. We all were.

Our family had shattered.

*

Or maybe it didn't start there at all.

Maybe it started in Valesham, a market town in a remote corner of the Sussex Downs, one of the most beautiful little towns I have ever seen.

It was my first parish, for my first flock, where I met my first love, stole my first kiss…

I was greeted by the whip-crack of rifle fire as I pulled into the wide yard at the front of the large, old farmhouse. The walls were antique red brick, beneath climbing roses in several intermingled shades of red, white, and pink. It had been the home of Wolsey family for several generations, long before Humphry had the first notion of being ordained. He had never made use of the vicarage, a far more modest building on the edge of the village, which had left it free for my use.

Three shots rang out, from the hop fields behind the house, before a silence fell, broken again by another salvo, this time of four shots. Isabella Wolsey, the Reverend's wife lurked on the front door step, with a cigarette. She hopped to her feet, to squeeze me in a hug.

"Has somebody offended him?" I asked.

Isabella chuckled. "No. His new toy was delivered yesterday."

"Toy?" I asked.

"A world war two rifle. Some Italian thing my brother found him."

"The kind Lee Harvey Oswald used?" I guessed.

She nodded. "I do believe Verona will be eager to be rescued from this eccentric new endeavour of his."

That was a duty I was more than happy to fulfil.

I had crushed on, longed for, and suffered fever hot dreams about women before, but I had never dared believe somebody felt the same before, or let go, and fallen for somebody. As soon as I had met Verona she had smiled at me like an old friend, soon, but since we had admitted what we felt, since she looked into my eyes, knew I was about to kiss her, and promised it would be okay if I did, every time she saw me, she had broken into this whole new smile, like she was trying not to laugh with surprise, this smile that sent my heart wild, and butterflies swarming in my belly. She smiled, and toyed with her hair, all at the same time.

I loved that smile, but I could never get used to it. I never got used to the smile that suggested she couldn't quite believe I was still so painfully lost in my love for her.

She smiled at me that morning, and I smiled back.

Verona was stood by the fence with a stop watch. Her father, a big, round, broad shouldered man, with an operatic air, was leaning over a shelf clamped over the fence, raising it to a carefully measured height, staring down the iron sights of an antique bolt action rifle, to water melons on a coconut shy, at a mark spray painted on the grass at the far end of the hop frames, down the slope of the field.

"Stand by!" Reverend Humphry declared. "And…"

The rifle cracked, and Verona started the clock. Two more shots, in a few seconds, and the clock stopped. Humphry looked down his binoculars.

"Well, that about does it," Humphry sighed.

"Found your conspiracy?" I asked.

"Far from it," Humphry admitted, making the rifle safe, and wiping his brow. "I think I just proved that I'm as fast a shot, and as good a shot, as Lee Harvey Oswald."

"Better even," Verona said, brightly. "He only hit twice, and you scored three, on two of the five melons."

I grinned at the priest. "Is this your new side line? International assassinations?"

"Only," Humphry laughed, "as a hobby."

"Griffin is taking me to buy a birthday present," Verona said.

Humphrey puffed out his cheeks. "Isn't that meant to be a surprise?"

"Verona has better taste than me," I admitted, "so I thought I better ask for some pointers."

"Or," Humphrey said, patting my shoulder, "you found an excuse for a few stolen hours."

Verona flushed. "That as well." She gripped my arm. "Shall we slip away before he asks any questions?"

I nodded. "I would hate for him to have entirely the right end of the stick about us."

"Ta ta, father dearest," Verona said, kissing Humphrey's cheek. "Don't wait up. We will eat out."

As we beat a hasty retreat Humphrey called after us.

"You best not have fun!" he shouted. "I'm getting pretty good with this!"

Humphrey was an odd soul. He had inherited quite an armoury and had a fascination with things that went crack and bang, the same way he had a fascination with model soldiers, but he had nothing in his soul that would dare hurt a fly. He was a man who couldn't use an anti-biotic without pausing to pray for the poor microbes he would end. His armoury was a museum, preserving machines, and letting them work only against paper targets, or water melons. (Isabella was a different matter and was more than happy to bring wood pigeon or pheasant to the table, by her own expertise with a long arm).

Verona rested her head on my shoulder as we walked away.

*

The flee market was busy. We paced between he stalls, seeking treasures amongst the silver and gold, on velvet display cushions. Verona lifted one from the cushion, a thick silver band, inlaid with ceramic, painted all the colours of a peacock's plume. She smiled and slipped it on a finger. It did not make it past the knuckle.

"Oh!" She muttered. "This one would need resizing, but I know a place." She slipped it onto her ring finger and held it up to me. "See. One size out, that should be an easy fix."

"You really like it?"

"I love it." Her eyes fell on mine. "We can afford it, can't we?"

I looked at the price tag, then at the woman behind the counter. "I don't suppose we could haggle you down twenty quid?"

"I could knock a tenner off," the woman sighed, "to see it find a good home."

I dug out my wallet and handed over the cash.

Verona grinned, aglow with joy, as she tried to slip the ring from her finger. Her smile faded, and the joy vanished. Her eyes widened. "Griffy!"

I took her hand; the ring was stuck in place.

"Sorry," she whispered.

"What…" My cheeks burned, and my heart stuttered. "What if we left it on this finger?"

"Then…" She scowled at me. "Don't be daft, do you want my father to think we are going to get married?"

I stared into her eyes. "What if we were?"

Verona blinked her expression melting as her eyes widened. "Then… are you joking?"

I shook my head. "No. I… was just wondering if you wanted to grow old with me?"

She burst into laughter and caught me in a kiss.

There are some kisses that can only exist in perfect moment. Kisses where the world around you both muffles and fades, to shadows and fog. Verona caught me in one such kiss. A kiss that made the world spin.

She broke from the kiss, and crushed me into a hug, crying into my shoulder.

That afternoon, as we drove home, Verona suddenly sat up, and pointed to the woods by the road, to the trees surrounded by a blanket of bluebells.

"There's a car park up here, can we pull in?" she asked.

"Why?"

"I know how I want to tell some friends!" she said, her smile bright.

We tucked the car away in the far corner of the car park, and Verona marched into the woods, gripping my hand tight, as she dragged me behind her. We followed the path through the woods, down into a steep valley, an ancient stone bridge crossed a wide, lumbering, river.

Verona perched on the side of the side of the bridge and posed for me to take some pictures on her phone, all of her showing off the ring. I stepped close and leant over to get a close up of the ring on her finger. She caught me before I stood, and guided me into her embrace, dangerously close.

Her kiss was a light brush of her lips against mine. She leant back, knowing that I would follow, opening her body language, in an invitation, letting my hands drift to her sides, our heartbeats falling into time, as the next kiss grew deeper, and deeper, until it was far more than a kiss. We made love for the fist time, to the sound of running water, and after, Verona sat on the bridge, clinging me to her, until I stopped shaking, murmuring, breathless and contented her scarlet cheeks burning mine.

This was how I wanted to spend the rest of my life.

*

Not long before Christmas I was on the motorway, driving out to collect Verona from university, and take her home. My phone danced in the cup holder, as Bob tried to ring me, over and over. I took the next exit, and parked in the services, to call her back.

The phone was answered on the second ring. "Griffin! Have you seen Dad?"

"Bob, what's going on?"

There was a hesitation.

"Dad's being weird," Bob said, cautiously. "Don't worry, I'm going to talk to him, but if he turns up at yours, keep out of his way, yeah? He's... not himself."

"I'm not there," I assured her. "I'm going to Verona's Pre-Crimbo party with her housemates and won't be home until tomorrow."

"Okay." Bob sounded relieved.

"Bob," I said, cautiously, "are you sure this isn't something you want me to talk to him about?"

Another awkward pause.

"No," Bob decided. "Look, he was saying some pretty weird stuff. I think he's breaking down a bit, and... you need to stay well away from him. Please. He's not himself."

"I could come home and..."

"No!" Bob said, in a fierce tone. "No. Please. Go and see Verona and stay safe. I can fix this."

I knew well enough not to argue with my sister when her words were flecked with spittle.

A few hours later I got to the modern end of terrace house where Verona lived with a few other students. There was washing up that nobody wanted to be responsible for, a few stains on everything, music played too loud, and good cheer in abundance. Verona took my hand and refused to let me go all night. She listened, worried, when I told her about Bob's call, and rang my sister back to read her the riot act but seemed convinced that Bob had it in hand.

"We can check on them tomorrow," she promised, "when we get home."

I kissed her hand. "Thank you."

She pointed to her cheek, then her lips. I kissed each in turn, lingering on the latter for good measure.

We spent most the party dissuading her friends from their plans for our wedding, then we went outside, and snuggled on a bench, watching the stars, and talking all night. We retired to bed in the early hours. We woke a few hours later to make love, slow and tender, for breakfast, before we faced the long drive to the Downs.

It was a crisp, cold, winter day. The sun hung low and pale in the sky, catching the frost and ice, the fresh snow, that covered the hop fields and seeming to set them ablaze in their sparkle and glow. We parked in a remote corner of the drive, away from the Wolsey family home, in the spiderweb of shadows cast by the skeletal trees.

Verona unclipped her seatbelt and slithered over to snuggle against me. "What do you want to do?"

"I better ring Bob," I said, "and maybe speak to Dad. I should find out what's going on."

"Okay." She slid onto my lap. "Do you want moral support, or do you want me to go and make sure the bed is nice warm?"

I laughed. "You can go and get some sleep. I'll join you when I can. If your parents aren't going to... you know..."

"My parents already have plans for grandchildren," Verona said, with a sly smile. "Maybe not yet, but we need practise."

She leant forwards and met me in a kiss.

There was whip crack of sound, the windscreen cracked around a hole, and a supersonic bowling ball slammed into my ribs. Verona grunted with pain, flinching away from me, her eyes losing their focus. I tried to understand if the blood on her sweater was hers, or mine, or both. Verona fell forwards, her body limp, her head resting against my chin.

"Vee?" I held onto her. "Vee, stay with me. Stay with me honey."

There was another crack. Her head jolted, as a bullet punched its way out of her face and sliced me across the throat. I gurgled on a scream, or a sob, or a cry of pain.

Verona fell sideways, landing against the door, leaving a smear. Her eyes were vacant, all their love, warmth, joy, and hope were gone. They stared with the eternal patience of death, her face slack and expressionless.

My father stood by the house, one of the Reverend's rifles in his hand.

I couldn't move. I don't know if it was some survival instinct, the shock of blood loss, or absolute horror, but I could not move at all. A coldness was flowing through me, filling me. I felt like I was sinking into ice water. The blood on my chest, and my throat was boiling hot.

My father lowered the rifle, then dropped it where he stood. He backed away, and broke into a run, away from the house, over the fence, and into the fields.

My vision blurred into darkness.

I prayed to my Lord for mercy. To make whatever came next swift and painless, and to let me wake for an eternity with Verona.

There were worse ways to spend the hereafter.

# ONE

Canon Debiere gestured for me to take a seat in one of the tall, deep, chairs of well-worn green leather, in his office. He was a tall, thin, man, well into his seventies, but still spry, with eyes that could boggle like ping pong balls, and a shock of white hair. He carried himself in a precise manner, as befitting his vestments. He was fussing with a tea set.

"You have yours black, I believe," he said, "with a slice of lemon?"

"If it is no trouble," I answered. "Thank you."

"Not at all." He poured me a dainty cup and settled at the desk with his own. "A little bird whispers to me that you have… made tentative steps towards falling in love."

"I am sorry sir," I began, my throat tightening, "but if this is because you think I have done anything improper…"

"Not at all." He mimed a toast with his cup. "I trust you to act with the decorum and honour worthy of your role. She is a good woman?"

"Delia is…" I struggled for the words. "She is unlike anybody I ever met."

Debiere weighed that for a moment and nodded. "It is good you are moving on. I hope it reflects in your confidence overall. I was hoping I might ask a favour of you, for an old friend as much as for me."

"I'm sorry?"

"Humphry Wolsey needs to take a leave of absence, to be fitted with a new hip," Debiere said, with the smile a cat might offer a cornered mouse. "One of the all singing and dancing, light weight ones. He will be off his feet, and out of commission for some time. He trusts few enough people with his parish but was worried the man he wants to hand the keys to, might not yet be ready." He cocked his head. "He worries you will never want to see his little town again."

I blinked. "Am I being asked or told."

"Asked, of course," Debiere assured me, "but… with a friendly shove in the right direction. I assured him you have been moving on and excelling, and I was confident you would not let him down."

Of course, I could not. "He asked for me?"

"You thought he would ask for anybody else?" Debiere looked me up and down. "He worries he will not be able to return to his duties. If he is to be a prisoner of retirement, I believe he will want to be in good company."

"You mean to say sir, I am… being assigned to the church?"

"You are being asked to cover for a few weeks," Debiere said, his tone even, "and you are being informed that in the future you may be asked to take over the duties full time, so you might… be sure of your answer."

I sipped my tea, deep in thought. "I see."

"Given your situation," Debiere said, softly, "I do not expect a quick, or easy answer."

I sat frozen, feeling my past pressing in around me. "I do not wish to let my friend down, but..."

"Think about it," Debiere told me. "For a day or two."

*

I sat with Delia on the sofa. She was leaning against me, her head on my shoulder. The television was on, but neither of us was paying the old movie much attention. Delia was watching my finger, as it traced little circles on her wrist.

"Will you go?" she asked.

"Would you come with me?" I corrected myself. "Could you? I know you have so much work, and..."

She took hold of my hand and held it to her cheek. "Do you think I would let you face this alone?"

I shook my head. "You are... a good friend."

"Is that all I am?" she whispered.

I shook my head again. "No. I know I have asked you to be patient with me, and to take this slowly, but I don't think we could ever just be friends. It would have to be all or nothing."

Delia bit her lip trying to resist saying aloud whatever the first thought in her head was. She looked at me, and her expression became sultry, and determined, her smile curling with mischief. "Why?" she whispered.

"Because you are beautiful," I answered.

"Mm?" She snuggled closer, moving her hand out of reach.

I drew a love heart on her knee with a fingertip. "Because my heart beats louder when you are near, and aches when I have to be without you."

"Mm?" She lay her fingers on my wrist, guiding my finger over the curve of her thigh.

"Because I want… I…"

"Because you like touching me laying against you?" she whispered.

"Yes."

"Because you like to touch me like this?" she asked, caressing my hand, as it caressed her thigh.

"Yes," I whispered, my heart racing.

"Because you want to kiss me?" she asked.

I cupped her chin, and gently angled her head to me. She did not resist. She closed her eyes, accepting my kiss. She pushed me back, leaning over me, hungrily, passionately, driving the kiss on. When we surfaced for air, she pecked my lip, signing the kiss, and let her lips remain against mine, as we panted for breath.

"Because," she whispered quietly, "nothing is not an option. Is it?"

"I…" I drew a breath. "I am completely…"

"I know." She kissed me again and smiled. "Me too." She settled back into my arms, as we explored each other with our touches, kisses, and caresses, letting our passions rise up, and boil over.

The knock at the door brought them to a sudden, halt.

"Now?" Delia gasped, looking to the ceiling. "Did I upset your boss somewhere down the road?"

I slithered out from under her and crept to the door. Helen stood in the hallway, looking like she was half a second from falling to pieces, her cheeks streaked with tears. She cried so hard her nose was running. She was dressed for a date, in a tight black sweater, and those flattering embroidered jeans of her. Her hair had been sculpted, and there was a little more effort in her make-up.

"Helen?" I stepped back to let her in. "What happened? I thought you were off for a weekend away with Bob?"

"So, did I," Helen muttered. "I... I dropped the kids off with their Nan, got dressed up, drove to hers, and... she hasn't shown. I've been sat outside her house for two hours now, trying to ring her, text her, poke her on the Social Stream."

"What about the Police station?" Delia asked.

I sat Helen down, and gave her a hug.

"She clocked off shift, and went home as normal," she said. "The desk sergeant is going to ring me if anybody knows anything, but... Griff, did you hear anything? Do you know how to reach her? Should I be worried?"

My heart went cold. I looked at Delia, she saw the truth behind my eyes, the yawning pit in my stomach. "I haven't heard anything. I have a key for her house. Shall we go see if there is any sign of something untoward?"

Helen nodded. "If you please?"

"Okay," Delia said, in a very serious tone. "Shall we?"

*

I eased open the front door, and we stepped into the hallway of Bob's house. All was still and quiet. I glanced down at the shoe rack by the door. Bob was a creature of habit. She went to work dressed in jeans and a comfy trainer and changed into her uniform at the station. Her scuffed and well-worn canvas trainers were by the door. Her favourite coat was hanging up. Her heavy boots, were gone, as was her padded leather jacket.

I flicked open the key safe. Her car keys were there, those for her bike were missing.

Delia followed me inside, her arm around Helen.

"Griffin?" Helen whispered.

Something felt wrong. There was a light shining through the glass door to the living room. I gestured for the others to wait and eased open the door. There was a cold breeze. I glanced around and took in a number of details at once. The draft came from the kitchen, where there were three neat holes in the window over the sink. There was a box of old electronics poured over the coffee table and discarded on the sofa. The light was from the screen of an old laptop, one old enough to have a DVD drive. It was plugged in, and a screensaver filled the screen with the image of a living aquarium.

There were bullet holes on the bookcase opposite the kitchen.

"Touch nothing," I said, quietly. "Dial nine nine nine."

"Bob?" Helen shouted. "Bob?"

Delia took out her phone and called the Police. I stepped carefully into the living room and took a pen from my pocket. There was a padded envelope cut open, laying by the computer, and a clear plastic case for a CD. I tapped the keyboard with my pen.

The computer span up to speed, and a video, whose quality suggested it was a good few years old, filled the screen. I set it playing with a tap of the pen.

Flo stared out of the screen. She was frail and ailing, struggling to breathe. "If you are watching this, then I am dead, and I owe my family an apology. Especially you Jack. I... couldn't do it. I couldn't face surviving to fight like this again, and again. I know... the HIV makes me vulnerable. The cancer will survive, and take root, and I will fight, and fight, but I won't... I won't live. Just fight or survive. I can't do that Jack. Somebody slipped me this." She held up a syringe. "With luck this video won't be found until long after I'm gone. I made arrangement with somebody to hide it, and only reveal it if there is a suspicion of foul play in my death, so I can prove that the one who supplied this did not kill me. It will my choice, by my own hand, and is not decided. I ask no action be taken against them. I forced their hand. I convinced them and held leverage over them. Only I should face the consequences of my choice, and I believe I will be in the hands of a power who will know how to judge me. I am sorry, Jack. Please. If you ever see this video, let me be the only one you need forgive."

Anger burned in my chest, so hot it became, for a moment, hate.

"No!" I snapped the word, louder than intended. "No, no, Flo…"

I stared at the envelope. I noted the local post mark over the stamps, and the neat copperplate handwriting. I knew my father's hand, as I knew he was the only one who would insist on calling my sister Robin instead of Bob.

I looked at the window, and the bullet holes.

Suddenly I was too afraid to feel anything else.

# TWO

"Your father?" DCI Salmon asked, as he paced around the interview room of the Police station.

"Yes." I stared at him. "Which means my sister is running from him, and in terrible danger."

"And how can you know it was him?" Salmon asked.

"The envelope. He sent her that disc. Then he tried to shoot her, to kill her, as he has killed before."

Salmon stopped pacing and leant on the table. "He has been missing a long time. Why resurface now? Where did he get another gun?"

"Bob has always been looking for him," I said. "Maybe she got close."

"And why would he shoot her?"

"I don't know!" I looked away. "I don't know why he would beat up the Reverend Wolsey or his wife, steal a rifle, and shoot their daughter." The words of the video stung me. "I didn't even know Flo had taken her own life."

"Neither did the coroner," Salmon admitted. "If she did, it went undetected. I am willing to admit the possibility, or that your father believed she had." He looked at me. "And I am willing to wonder if he saw this video, all those years ago, and thought he knew who helped Flo die. Is your father a vengeful sort?"

Anger flared in my stomach once more. "And you think now he might believe it of Bob?"

"Is it a possibility?" Salmon asked.

"No!" I held up my hands. "No! You know her! You work with her! How can it be a possibility?"

"Is it a possibility," Salmon asked, slower, "that your father, or somebody acting on his behalf believes it?"

"He murdered Verona," I whispered. "I don't know what he is capable of believing. Where is my sister?"

"There was no blood," Salmon said. "Her house has a garden, then there is an alley, on the other side of which, is the back of a shop. We think he was on the fire escape. The bullets suggest a rifle. We can assume she is unharmed, and seeing as her bike, helmet, and boots are gone, we are looking for her on the motorbike. We will find her."

*

Delia and I escorted Helen back to her front door. It was so late it was almost early. We hovered in the hallway.

"Helen," I said gently. "Maybe you should go and join the Trouble with your mother for a few days?"

"No." Helen shook her head. "If Bob tries to send me word, or needs somewhere safe, I should be here."

Delia frowned a little. "I think Bob would want you to be safe."

"Yeah?" Helen chuckled. "Well, she kissed me, which makes me her girlfriend, which is bad news, as I'm pretty intent on being the one she needs, not the one she wants." Her chuckle became a sob. "And I don't think I can handle the idea that it's too dangerous to be here for her. You think I see your scars and think I have to run? That is why I need to be here, so she can find me!"

Delia hugged her. "We are right across the hall."

We bid her goodnight and retired to my own flat.

Delia wrapped her arms around me. "Hey."

"Hey." I flushed. "So... you should probably stay over."

She smiled. "I thought so."

"I can sleep on the sofa, if..." I flustered a little, as her lips brushed my neck.

"No." Delia took my hand. "I am not letting you out of my sight."

I kissed her forehead. Her cheeks blossomed. She closed her eyes, as we both leant into the next kiss.

"Completely," I whispered.

"What?" She giggled.

"Earlier I tried to tell you I was completely in love with you."

"And I told you I know," she purred.

"Utterly and completely," I whispered. "I am completely and utterly in love with you, which is scary because..."

"I know." She held on to me. "I feel it too. I don't know how to say it, but I can show you. I can bake you a cake, or choose the perfect date for us, or…" She breathed out. "Or I can stay. With you. Even tonight. Just to feel a little safer."

Her smile was hopeful. It melted my heart, and for a moment I forgot how to breathe, or talk, or do anything but stare into her eyes.

A feeling flooded me. Something I had not felt in years. Something I had never thought I could feel so strongly. Even for Verona.

Delia oozed into the embrace. "It's okay. It scares me too. It shouldn't be this fast, this strong, this…" She kissed my cheek. "Perfect. I don't want anything. Just not to be alone. Just to sleep. Just to be with you."

I took her hand and guided her to the bed.

Our sleep was broken, but we were content to lay there, basking in our shared warmth, my fingers tracing the curve of her back, as we curled against each other. She sighed softly, as she ebbed in and out of her dreams.

*

The next morning, I rose early to make coffee and French toast, while Delia showered. She stepped out of the bathroom, wearing a borrowed tee shirt that was appealing tight against her ample frame. She was without makeup, her wet hair hanging loose, her beauty all of her own, in her smile, in her eyes, in the way she leant on the counter and watched me cook.

"What?" she asked, her voice husky.

"You…" I stepped over, and put my arms around her, resting my hands on the counter either side of her hips. "You are beautiful."

"You really mean that, don't you?"

Her hands were on my sides. She took hold of my belt and pulled me closer. "So, what we were about to do yesterday?"

"Oh?" I asked. Nuzzling her neck with fluttering kisses.

"And how I said, I'm not that good with words," she whispered, "but want to show you how I feel?" She rolled her head back on her neck, exposing the spot she liked me to tickle. My kisses made her purr. "Oh God. What were those other kinds of massage you knew?"

I slid my hands under her tee shirt.

There was a knock on the door.

She looked up to the ceiling. "What? Is this a test?"

"If it is, you are passing," I promised, drawing away with a kiss to the cheek. "I'm yours forever. We have all the time we need."

The knock repeated at the door.

"Yes?" I asked.

"Mister Barley?" DCI Salmon asked. "If you don't mind?"

"Reverend Barley!" I said, walking to the door. "I did not spend years in a theological college to be a Mister Barley."

I opened the door. DCI Salmon stared past me, at Delia.

"Oh?" Salmon asked. "Really?"

My heart ran fast. "Is there news, Detective Chief Inspector? Is my sister safe?"

"That is something I am hoping you can tell me," he said, his tone blunt. "We found her motorbike, and a message. I need you to tell me what the message means. Get your coat."

*

We drove across the city, to Howes Common, a borough in the South East of London. It was one of the small towns gobbled up as London expanded, oozing ever outwards. It was where Bob and I grew up, and despite the best efforts of the redevelopment projects, it still looked grotty, with too much litter, and patterns of dirt left by the rain.

The Oaken Man was a shell of a pub, burned out when I was twelve (coincidentally when the owners needed the insurance money), but had never been rebuilt, which was generally considered something of an improvement. When I was fifteen it had been the hang out for the local kids, or at the least for Bob, and a few of her friends. Which meant I, having nobody else, washed up there often enough.

The motorbike was parked amongst the rubble, to one side of the roofless husk, where the bar had once stood. Bob's leather jacket, helmet, and boots were with it. The wall was covered with graffiti, a dozen different murals, and tags, all overlapping and blotting each other out. Bob's old tag was over the rest, like a postage stamp for the stencilled missive next to it.

Forensics Officers, in white paper overalls were marking evidence and taking photographs. They emptied the remnants of a small bonfire from a waste paper bucket into clear plastic bags. The stencils, and other papers, pages of coral pink lined paper, with spidery writing in red ball point pen.

Flo's paper.

Flo's hand writing, from her favourite pen.

I looked at the message. "The Shriving Time is nigh. Meet me where angels fear."

"Does that mean something to you?" Salmon asked.

I took a picture with my phone. "It's interesting."

"Oh, a lot here is interesting," Salmon whispered.

"Like how she managed to carry a waste paper bin here?" I asked. "It seems a bit awkward for a motorbike doesn't it?"

Salmon nodded. "And I assume she had other shoes? If she left her boots?"

Dark thoughts drained the colour from my world. "And the stencils? Why would she have had the stencils ready? Was she planning this?"

Salmon puffed out his cheeks. "Does the message mean anything to you?"

"Shriving time is a period of mercy, to allow one to make their peace, and seek atonement, before they are put to death," I said. "Where Angels Fear was... a name for Cinderoak. Bob had a friend from class, who lived in the tower. They used to hang out up on the roof. There was graffiti up there. Nobody ever knew who put it there, a beautiful mural with those words. May I see the letters please? From the fire?"

Salmon got a Forensic technician to bring them over, in their plastic bags. I stared at the letters and read what was left of them.

The one I was handed, from the language, was to her priest, asking his forgiveness for her not having the strength to go on, and for the way she passed. She hoped Reverend Miller (who had long since passed through the veil himself) would know his words and his kindness had always inspired her.

I looked through the others as they were collected. Letters to my father, to me, to Flo's other friends (a pair of chefs living in the South of France, her next-door neighbour, and guy she had coffee with every Thursday afternoon), all offering goodbyes, and promising she did not choose to die easily.

Salmon cleared his throat. "Is it not convenient," he said, "that they were all burned, and yet enough survived for us to know who they were for?"

"There is no letter for Bob," I whispered.

Salmon nodded. "I see. Why don't you show me this spot in Cinderoak?"

"We need to check somewhere first," I told him.

He looked at me.

"My lock up," I said. "Bob keeps some stuff there."

Salmon nodded.

*

My lock up was under a railway arch, in Gallows Cross. A train rumbled overhead as I unlocked the door and pulled them open. There was a bare square on the concrete where my car had been stored. I flicked on the lights and checked the storage lockers at the side of the room.

The lockers she had claimed were empty.

Bob's phone lay broken on the floor, the SIM card destroyed.

"What's missing?" Salmon asked.

"My car. She's insured on it, and I kept the MOT up to date, you know, just in case."

Salmon nodded. "Okay. Anything else?"

"She put stuff in here when she moved," I said, "and never had time to take it to her house. Clothes, her fishing stuff, a camp bed, tent, a couple of kit bags."

"A change of clothes, and a car," Salmon said. "A good start if you need to get out of the city. Any ideas where she might be going?"

I gave him a helpless look. "Her best friends are the ones she shared a section house with, when she was new in the Force. Drake, Slater, Flex?"

Salmon gave me a look. He had already tried them. "If she is running, who wants you at Cinderoak?"

I shrugged. "Shall we find out?"

# THREE

I stepped out of the access stairs and onto the roof of Cinderoak tower. A squall of bitter cold wind billowed around me. Salmon followed, keeping as close to the wall, and as far from the edge, as he could. He stepped away to look at the graffiti that covered the wall of the stair well. An angel and demon, built like superheroes, hacked at each other with broadswords, against a vista of burning buildings, and the highly stylised legend: "Where Angels Fear."

There was the shrill ring of a mobile phone.

I followed the sound to the edge, to the barrier topped with a handrail, and leant over to take a look. It was a long way down to the car park. My stomach knotted. My heart lurched to my throat. There was a cheap pay-as-you-go mobile phone stuck to the back of the panel, by silver cloth tape. I pulled it free and showed it to Salmon. He took the phone and answered the call.

"Hello?" he asked.

The phone clicked off.

It rang again.

"Hello?" Salmon said, answering the phone. "Don't go!"

The line went dead.

It rang again.

I took the phone from him and answered. "It's me."

There was a sharp breath. It wasn't Bob.

I walked back to the handrail. "Reverend Griffin Charles Barley speaking."

"Griffin," my father said. "Do not hang up the phone, and do not pass me to whoever else that is. A policeman? One of her colleagues?"

I looked around, and down, scanning the parks and squares for signs of my father.

"DCI Salmon," I said, carefully. "Dad, did you try and murder Bob?"

There was a pause. "Don't call her that. Her name is Robin. How many times do you have to be told?"

"None, because you are wrong. Did you try and murder Bob?"

"I tried to kill her," my father stated, over the line. "I'm not so sure it would be murder."

"No? Why don't you meet me and Salmon for a coffee?" I smiled. "I am sure the Metropolitan Police would be glad to tell you when shooting somebody with a rifle is murder."

There was a glint of light on the roof of the tower across the way. It could have been my imagination, but it looked a lot like the sun reflecting on a lens. Maybe binoculars, or a telescopic scope. Dread filled my body and slowed my heartbeat to a crawl.

"Do not argue with me," dad sneered. "That leads to more deaths."

"That sounds a lot like murder," I whispered.

Salmon followed my gaze and nodded.

"I should warn you, I have a rifle aimed at you," dad said. "Keep that in mind before you talk. I will not hesitate to kill you."

"Like you killed Verona?"

"That was regrettable," he snapped.

"Then like you tried to kill me?"

"That was..." He hesitated. "That was also regrettable. I thought you had... I thought it was you."

"It was me?" I could taste the bile in my words. "That killed Flo you mean?"

"Yes. I thought you murdered my sister." His tone was low and saddened. "I was wrong. Now I know better."

"Now you are framing Bob," I said, coldly. "I assume it was you who left her bike, and spray painted a message, for us? You left the letters to be discovered. Did you destroy Bob's letter?"

"No." He drew a breath. "I will ensure it goes to the police. For DCI Salmon's attention?"

"Why are you trying to frame her?"

"I am not." Dad seethed. "It was her. I thought it was you. I was wrong. I found the letters. I read Flo's message to her. I knew I was wrong."

The world span about me. "I do not believe it. You were wrong before. Why don't you prove it to me? Bring me the letter, explain it to us, and I will ensure Salmon finds Bob and if she betrayed us, she will answer for her actions."

"No." Father snapped. "No. That is not what is going to happen. You are going to help me find her, or... I will be forced to hurt others. Your fat friend from the cupcake shop. Or the whore that Bob has been rutting with."

I shook my head. "No! Dad! Whatever you are doing, killing the people I love, and Bob loves, will never be the answer! Please. We can do this right."

"She killed my sister!" Dad screamed. "She made me murder an innocent woman! She made me try to kill my own son! She let me believe you deserved to die! If the others die, it will be because she made this all happen!"

"You need help," I whispered. "Please. If you love any of us, hand yourself in, and let me get you help."

"Where would she go?" Dad demanded.

"She has nowhere," I whispered.

"She isn't hiding from me!" Dad snapped. "She is hiding from you, Griffin. Where would she go?" His tone hardened. "Where would you never go?"

"I don't know!" I hissed.

"You have two hours to change that," Dad muttered, and cut off the line.

For twenty long seconds, I was numb. I was lost in a cold fog, frozen in place, as Salmon barked into his phone, sending officers to my flat, and to Helen, to find them, to protect them, to send somebody to the other tower, in response to an armed and dangerous fugitive.

He waved a hand before my eyes. "Hey! Hey! Are you okay there, Barley?"

I snapped back to reality, with a nauseous jolt. "Delia. I have to check she's okay."

"Officers are on their way to her," Salmon said. "I need that mobile."

"I can't," I said, firmly. "If my father tries to ring it, and I don't answer..."

"I need it," Salmon said, "for the number that rang us, so I can stop your father hurting your friends."

I handed him the phone and took out my own. Delia answered in a few rings.

"Hey," she said, in a hurry. "Are you okay?"

"The Police are on their way to you and to Helen," I said, quietly. "DCI Salmon is sending them to keep you all safe. My father just... he threatened you, if I don't help him find Bob."

Delia drew a breath. "Are you okay?"

"I don't..." I rubbed my head. "I don't know where Bob would hide. If she didn't go to her Police friends, I don't know where she is."

"Griffin," Delia said softly, "please, tell me you are going to be okay?"

"You are going to be safe," I said. "The Police are going to look after you, and Helen, and her kids. You are going to be safe, and that means, whatever happens, I'm going to be okay."

There was sound that might have been her swallowing.

"I love you," she whispered. "I am crazy deep in love with you, already."

"I love you too," I said, softly. "I don't want to lose you. For a few weeks while I work away. Forever if I have to move. I... want to be with you. If... if you would have me?"

"I want that too," Delia whispered. "I want that too."

*

I sat in Salmon's car, watching the road go by, as he drove.

"Where would your father get a gun?" The DCI asked.

"Last time he beat up my friends and stole one of their rifles."

Salmon looked at me. "Think he went back there?"

I took out my phone and thumbed open a number.

"Hello?" Isabella Wolsey enquired.

"Hey," I said. "It's..."

"Griffin!" She cooed. "You are ringing because of the Humphrey's operation? You will be here for him?"

"Actually," I said quietly, "I wanted to check you were okay. My Dad is... back... and he has a rifle, and..."

"You think he is coming here?" she asked.

"No. I worried he went to you to steal a rifle."

"He will not show his face here," Isabella whispered. "He knows that if he tries, if he comes anywhere close to here, I will shoot him where he stands, clean between the eyes."

Dad was wrong. Bob wouldn't run where I couldn't find her. She would run where he wouldn't dare look for her.

I cleared my throat. "Is my sister okay?"

There was a long pause. No bemused laugh, or confused splutter, no asking me what I meant.

"Isabella," I said, firmly, "is my sister there?"

"Yes," Isabella said.

Salmon stared me, agape.

"Would it be okay if I came to talk to her?" I asked.

"Of course," Isabella said gently. "If that is what it takes to bring you back here, of course."

# FOUR

Salmon pulled over to the side of the road and stared at me long and hard.

"Where do you think you are going to go?" he asked, his tone still as plate glass.

"Sussex." I put my phone back in my pocket. "My sister is staying with old friends, in the Parish I am due to babysit soon."

"And did somebody mention shooting your father?" Salmon asked.

"When he shot me, he shot their daughter," I said, gently, "the woman I was going to marry. She did not survive. If life was fair, I would be dead, she would have lived, and gone on to find somebody else, and... he would have thought all this was over."

"Will they do it?" Salmon asked.

"Humphrey collects and studies antique firearms. He is something of an expert in the field. Isabella shoots birds, with a rifle, and with shot, all licensed and above board. I understand her anger, and she has the means to defend herself, but I do not think either would seek to shed blood. They are not built for hate."

"A murdered daughter changes somebody," Salmon said, with the weight of experience. "Look at what grief and loss did to your father. Can you convince Bob to come in and talk to us?"

"Will my friends be safe?" I asked.

"We will protect them," Salmon assured me. "The question is if your dad will follow you south, to catch Bob, or if he will hang around here looking for a way to make good on his threat. At least if we go to find Bob, he will think you are working towards what he asked of you." He tapped open his satellite navigation. "Now, where are we going?"

*

We stopped for petrol in a garage on the A road, at the edge of Valesham. I sat in the car while Salmon filled up and went inside. He ducked into the back of the garage, out of view and into the toilets.

On the back seat, the phone from my father began to ring. I reached over and scooped it up.

"Hey Dad," I said, "where are you watching me?"

There was an awkward silence for a heartbeat. "Why do you say that?"

"Because," I said firmly, "otherwise it would be too much of a coincidence that you happened to ring when my Police escort was out of the way." I looked around, trying to spot my father, in a car, or a van, parked somewhere nearby. I couldn't spot him. "Are you satisfied I am working on what you want?"

"You realise that if the Reverend or his Italian bombshell are protecting her, they will die?" He spoke in a sharp tone. "I need you to talk to them. To draw Bob out, alone, to the field behind the house. Now. Right now. Drive away and do it now."

"We sent word to the local constabulary," I said. "There are Police officers at the house."

"No. Your little Piggy is too smart for that. He doesn't want Bob to run. You didn't even warn her you were bringing a friend to the party. You wanted to speak to her, before I knew where you were looking."

I tried to act like panic was not burning my veins and continued to look for my father amongst the traffic and bustle. I noted Salmon was in the queue, and on his way to paying for the petrol. "Dad, you can still stop this, without spilling any more blood."

He grunted.

I felt my voice harden. "The man I knew would never try to make his family party to murder."

"Then how about justice?"

"What you want is not justice," I said, firmly.

"You," he snorted, "are the one who believes in a God who wants an eye for an eye. You are the one whose faith is in a book that would stone a woman to death for far less terrible crimes than your sister committed."

"I also believe in the parts that say one should not kill, or that there can be forgiveness, redemption, and hope," I warned him. "Come to the car. Let me talk to you in person, and I will see you get help."

"You are trying my patience."

There was the zip of a silenced bullet.

Something chipped the kerb of the island, by the petrol pump.

My father's voice was ice cold. "My next shot will hit DCI Salmon. After that I start aiming at petrol pumps. People die, if you do not do as you are told, Griffin."

I slid into the driver's seat, and drove away, the phone still to my ear. "I'm going. I'm going!"

"Good." Father's tone softened. "A wise decision."

I followed the main road, leaving Salmon to run out onto the forecourt, screaming impotently after me. I tried to keep my voice level. "He's going to send the police ahead of us."

A dark van pulled out onto the road, several cars behind me.

"Of course, he will," my father agreed. "And they will cause more bloodshed. If you wish to save lives, time is of the essence."

I approached a roundabout.

My father chuckled on the phone. "Ah. Don't you dare think about turning right, for the Police station. Stay in lane and drive to our pretty house with the roses."

I did as I was instructed. "Do you know what you did to me?"

"What your sister allowed to happen?" father demanded.

"Her finger was not on the trigger," I said, evenly, as I joined the road out of town and into the hop fields. "She did not choose to shoot at me and Verona. She did not choose to pull a trigger. She did not flee, without offering medical help."

"I didn't…" My father choked on his answer. "I could only see the shadow moving. In your car. In the driver's seat. I have had to live with what I did to Verona too long."

"Do you understand what you did?" I asked.

"I know I killed her." Dad drew a breath. "I have seen death. I was a soldier. I saw death in the line of duty. I saw my sister die."

"Flo chose to take her own life," I said. "You chose to take others. You have seen death, but did you ever see the person you murdered die?"

"I murdered nobody," my father said, too quickly to believe his words. "Her death was unfortunate, a mistake, but I am not a murderer."

"Do you know what it is to see the life fade from her eyes?" I asked. "To feel her turn from the person you loved, and I do still love my Verona, nothing will ever change that, to a thing of meat and bone and blood?"

"Shut up!" my father shouted.

We were almost at the house. I could see the roof looming above the trees.

"Do you understand what you are making me a part of?" I asked.

We were alone on the road. It was just me and the black van.

I slammed on the brakes.

"What are you doing?" The voice on the phone demanded, as the van screeched to a stop beside me.

I threw the car into reverse and stamped the accelerator into the carpet. The car screamed backwards, and into the nose of the van with a crunch of metal on metal, and breaking glass.

My ears rang, and the world span about me, muffled in a sickening soft focus. I stumbled out the door.

My father fell out of the van, clutching a rifle with a long silencer on the barrel. He lifted the butt to his shoulder, and held it ready to fire, pointing the barrel at me. He panted for breath.

"You can kill me," I said. "Then what? The police are on their way. They will swarm the area. You will be caught before you reach town. Before you can hurt anybody."

He shook his head. "Get out my way."

"No."

His finger took the slack off the trigger. "Step aside or die."

"Death is easier to face than helping you kill," I said. "I am better prepared for it."

He swore under his breath, as sirens filled the air around us.

I stepped towards him. "If you won't kill me, put the gun down."

The barrel of the gun flashed, with a sound like heavy books falling, but not like a rifle shot. Something that felt like an express train hit me in the side and there was suddenly ice-cold pins and needles where I used to be able to feel my legs. I landed against the car with a thump and tried to stay upright.

My father stood still, looking at me, as though not understanding what he had done to me. He was older, darker, and leaner than I had known him, shaven scalped, with deeper, darker, eyes. He opened his mouth to say something but couldn't.

"Don't," I gasped. "Please don't."

The words hurt. Breathing hurt.

I slid down the car, leaving a bloody streak. The world was filling with pain, and the sound of my own heart.

He leant on the car beside me. "You won't let me do this," he said, "but I can't live with it this way. With Flo dying for nothing. With you, and with Verona. I have to. I have to or far too much has happened for no reason. I'm too deep to stop, because if I stop it was all for nought, and it will all still burn in me. I have to keep on going until I make it right."

"There isn't a life you can take," I gasped, through the pain, "that could ever make this right. All you do, is make more people know your pain, your bile. It has to stop. Just stop."

He nodded. "Maybe there is one life," he whispered.

"No!" I tried to grab the gun from him, but it was too late.

The gun thumped. He fell away.

I closed my eyes, so I did not have to see.

# EPILOGUE

Bob watched me fighting my way across the prison visiting room, with my crutches. She looked sickly, tired, and haggard, but was still more beautiful than I could ever be. Her smile was thin, and her hands were shaking.

Delia helped me down into the chair and rested her hand on my shoulder.

"Griffin and Dee," Bob said, with a smile. "I'm… getting used to this. It's like I expect to see one of you, and there you both are. Always together, like you have always been together." She looked at Delia. "Are you looking after him?"

Delia nodded. Her smile was more polite than genuine.

"I shouldn't have run," Bob whispered. "I thought I was taking the danger away from you. I thought I was protecting Helen. She… she's okay?"

"She is trying to understand what happened," I said, "and why."

"She's trying to work out if I helped Flo die?" Bob nodded. "It's fair. I guess she has to know now. You all do. I… helped her. Hospital security is a joke. Tired doctors, losing track of things, distracted by jobs here and there? It was too easy to swipe a syringe and prime it for her. When she didn't have the strength to do it herself, I put it in her drip, and let her slip away. There was no reason to suspect I had been there, and nobody suspected foul play, so nobody checked the tapes back. Dad found the message years ago. He figured it was you. It broke him. I… couldn't make myself tell you the truth. You needed me more than you needed the truth. You needed your sister."

I stared at her. "You did the action?"

Bob shook her head. "What else could I do? She was suffering. If it was one of our rats, or hamsters, we would have given her peace. It was less cruel, because she chose it to happen. She understood why, and she knew life was… A few years later and it wouldn't have mattered. She could have gone abroad to a clinic and done it legally. At the time? Her hands were tied, and I offered her the mercy you couldn't. I won't be sorry for that."

I closed my eyes. "You just… you…"

"I carried on." She met my eyes. "Life had to carry on. Flo was sure of that."

"You should have spoken to me," I said. "We could have found another way. We could have…"

"We could have, what?" Bob asked, knowing there was no easy answer.

"You could have warned me," I said. "You could have told me what dad thought I had done."

"And then what?" Bob smiled and held my hands, tears on her cheeks. "You would have saved me? Or Verona? Dad?"

"I would have tried!" My fingers grabbed hers, the knuckles bleaching. "I could have tried."

"I know." Bob leant over and kissed my cheek. "I should have warned you, and you could have tried. You always try, but I thought I could talk dad down. I thought I could make it right. I... I was going to tell him, the whole truth, but then it suddenly didn't matter anymore. He had broken everything." She looked away. "So, I buried it deep, and I became the better me."

I shook my head.

"No." Bob laughed. "I don't believe that either, but... what else do I have to try and believe?"

I raised an eyebrow.

"Oh." She nodded. "Okay. There is that, I suppose."

Delia squeezed my shoulder.

"I'm not giving up on you." I stared at my sister. "Whatever happens at trial, I am going to help you through this."

Bob shrugged. "Why?"

"Because," Delia said, softly, "he's still family."

Bob nodded. "Okay. Well... you can't make it any worse, can you?"

*

We sat in the car, in silence for several long minutes before we left the prison.

"So…" Delia cleared her throat. "I was thinking…"

"Oh?" I enquired.

"Maybe we didn't go home, tonight." She stared at my eyes, wearing my favourite smile. "Maybe we go find a bed and breakfast in the countryside, and spend all day, all night, just… together. Doing whatever happens. If… you know… you are recovered enough from surgery for a little gentle exertion."

"I think I could manage to give you a foot rub."

"That is a good start," she said. "And if… nobody interferes, maybe we could… do more?"

I nodded. "Why, do you know a place?"

"A very nice place," she said. "It's kind of remote."

"In the countryside?"

"In Scotland." She chewed her lip. "Gretna Green?"

I stared at her.

She raised an eyebrow. "Hey, just because we don't have to hurry, doesn't mean we can't…"

I nodded. "Okay."

She smiled. "Really?"

I nodded again. "We have our whole lives together. Let's start now."

She leant over to kiss me.

It was the kind of kiss that was the start of a whole new life.

# More by TE Hodden

What Once Went Wrong

Labyrinth House

Uncanny London (A Fallowgrave Tale)

Threadbare Hearts Presents: Anthology Vol.1